William Carew Hazlitt

Montagu and Co.

An original comedy in four acts

William Carew Hazlitt

Montagu and Co.
An original comedy in four acts

ISBN/EAN: 9783337049003

Printed in Europe, USA, Canada, Australia, Japan

Cover: Foto ©Andreas Hilbeck / pixelio.de

More available books at **www.hansebooks.com**

MONTAGU AND CO.

AN ORIGINAL COMEDY

IN FOUR ACTS

BY

William CAREW HAZLITT

LONDON
GEORGE REDWAY
1897

MONTAGU AND CO.

Scene.—London, Rotterdam, and Streatham.
Time.—The Present.

ACT I.

Scene 1.

A man-servant in black clothes discovered standing with folded arms at the back of a chair near the table to L. *in a dining-room furnished in the usual style. A looking-glass over the mantel-piece and oil-paintings round the room.*

Serv. (*unfolding his arms and coming forward a little*). Well, I don't understand that saying, "Be-tween two stools a man comes to the ground." A man doesn't come to the ground any more because he's between two stools. Therefore it is nonsense: therefore it is impossible: therefore it means something else: therefore it means, "Between two *fools* a man comes to the ground." I know who the two fools are—they're my masters;

A

and as for the man, that's me.   The saying is, "Two of a trade never agree;" no more do my two masters; they're always at it.   There's my young master has no money, and my old master says that he hasn't any.   A pretty dilemma for me, with a name to keep up!   But, Lord bless me! as the quarters come round, the tin comes in : and what I say is, that there must be gold-diggings in the coal-cellar, or Mr. Percival the Helder, as we call him for short, is what I should name a humorous humbug.   There's a good deal about Mr. Percival the Helder which, if I was an empanelled jury of my countrymen, would strike me as ridic'lous affectation.   But I hear Mr. Percival the Junior's footstep.

Enter CHARLES PERCIVAL *in morning dress from* R.
SERV. *retires slowly up.*

CHAS. P. A-hem !

SERV. (*hurrying forward*). Yes, sir.

CHAS. P. Post ?

SERV. No, sir.

CHAS. P. Damn !

SERV. 'Least, I mean there's a goodish few, accordin' to habitude, from Mr. Percival the Senior, sir.

CHAS. P. Damn !

SERV. Yes, sir.

CHAS. P. Breakfast?

SERV. In the study, sir.

CHAS. P. Ah, that'll do.

SERV. Yes, sir.   [*Exit* SERV. L.

CHAS. P. (*throwing himself into a chair*). Dear, dear! 'tis only twelve, and here are six letters, special messages, telegrams, and the devil knows what, from my uncle. He's what they call a good-hearted sort of fellow, that is, he does the right thing when his esteemed nephew, the present deponent, has the slightest possible difficulty in regulating the balance between supply and demand until something turns up, has one foot in Bedlam and the other in the Bankruptcy Court with worry and duns. He occupies a room in my house till I'm married,—or he is. He is a gay old bachelor, and I'm a melancholy young bachelor. Yet why should I be melancholy, pshaw? The question is, why shouldn't I?——

Eh?   *Enter* SERVANT.

SERV. Letter for you, sir. (*Aside.*) From the old gentleman. What a rum fist he writes, too! Wonder, poor gentleman, whether he was hard up for a pen and used his toothpick?   [*Exit.*

CHAS. P. Good heavens! another despatch from my uncle—this makes seven. (*Holds it in his hand.*) First, let me see, he was coming home to-night; then he wasn't; then he thought that he should go to the theatre, and we were not to lock the street-door; then he thought that he should enjoy a turn at backgammon, and he would be with me punctually at eight; then he made up his mind (for the eight-and-fortieth part of a solar day) to run down to Blackheath, and see whether a sniff of the country air wouldn't take away that odd feeling he had in his left thumb; then he recollected that he had forgotten his portmanteau, and had only sixpence in his pocket, and resolved (for precisely thirty minutes, I'll lay a wager) to go half-price to the play, if he could borrow a clean collar from Chaffers, and two shillings and fourpence from somebody else. (*Opens the letter.*) Let us see what's the latest change in the temperature. (*Reads.*) "MY DEAR CHARLES,—Your situation is truly distressing. I should recommend you to look out for a nice room somewhere, where you can manage to live on—say, thirty shillings a week" (Wonder he didn't make it *a month*) "till things look brighter. For my own part, I have asked some people to take chambers for me in the Temple, and to arrange so that I may pay for the necessary furniture by easy instalments. I have borrowed a pound and a shirt of Jones, and shall go to Brighton by the afternoon train. I may return on Friday; but if you can let my

room to a desirable person on more advantageous
terms, I can easily manage to go elsewhere.—Your
affectionate uncle, H. PERCIVAL." What an extraordinary effusion! I wish I had some one to
lay odds with that the next, which is due in forty-
three minutes, will come by special messenger, and
contradict every word of this. (*Gets up and rings
the bell.*)

Enter SERVANT.

CHAS. P. Go over to the Clarence, where Colonel
Honeywood is stopping, and tell him that, as my
uncle does not return to-night, I can give him
a bed. He mayn't be up yet, for these military
chaps are late dogs.

SERV. Wouldn't it be more grammatical, Mr.
Charles, asking your pardon, to say, *these military
dogs are late chaps?*

CHAS. P. As why?

SERV. It'd take too long to explain my reasons,
Mr. Charles, so s'ppose I write them out.

CHAS. P. There, be off, and—I had almost forgotten what I was talking about.

SERV. Yes, sir.

CHAS. P. Oh, I remember;—tell the Colonel
that I shall be happy to see him here about a little
matter.

SERV. Wouldn't it be better to pretend, Mr.
Charles, that it's a *great* matter? Perhaps he won't

come if I say it's only a *little* matter. You can let the cat out of the bag when ye get him here.

CHAS. P. Have done! have done! [*Exit* SERV.

Enter COLONEL HONEYWOOD, *ushered in by* SERV.

SERV. (*aside*). Well, I *was* right; he *is* a military dog by his hair.   [*Exit.*

COL. H. Ah, my dear fellow, most fortunate; I was just coming over.

CHAS. P. Very glad to see you, Colonel; you were one of my poor father's friends (*they both dash away a tear, the* COLONEL *following suit*). Breakfasted yet?

COL. H. (*eagerly*). No, by Jove! I thought there was something. I'll go back, and——

CHAS. P. Couldn't think of such a thing, my dear sir. *I* haven't breakfasted.

COL. H. Most singular!

CHAS. P. You'll take a bit with me presently; it's laid in the study.

COL. H. Charmed, am sure.

CHAS. P. But there was a matter on which I wanted first to take your advice. (*The* COLONEL *bows acquiescence.*) I hope that you won't be offended if—if I mention to you that—I—I—in fact, that I am desirous of getting married!

COL. H. *Offended*, my dear fellow! Why should I be? Delighted to hear of your resolution. Girl with a little money, perhaps, and handsome, I'll swear, into the bargain! Ah! that's where you young dogs have us poor old fellows. Why, the girls won't look at me now. Gave up looking at me ever since they found out that I hadn't saved money in the Punjaub, and had three grey hairs in my left whisker. Heigho! (CHAS. P. *looks rather confused and blushes.*) Not what we should call a fortune, Charlie, eh? (COL. H. *hums an air and twirls his moustaches indifferently.*)

CHAS. P. (*mysteriously*). Well, perhaps so—perhaps not; and the fact is, between you and me, that—that the lady has been asked, but—but——

COL. H. Her papa and mamma have not, eh? Haven't I hit the nail on the head? But what can I do, my boy?

CHAS. P. Well, I don't mind telling you that it's the daughter of some people of the name of Montagu.

COL. H. Montagu! Montagu! Not old Cecil Montagu, of Montagu Brothers, London and Rotterdam?

CHAS. P. (*nervously*). Yes, the same.

COL. H. Why, they're one of the richest houses in England, and Cecil is the head of the firm. They've only one daughter. I know Montagu well, and his wife, too. I confess I could never make out why they hadn't half the peerage on the hungry look-out for Cecilia; but they don't see much company somehow. Mrs. M. is——

Chas. P. I don't like her altogether so well as I could wish to do.

Col. H. (*confidentially*). Insincere.

Chas. P. Just so.

Col. H. Rather a flirt still.

Chas. P. I don't know but what she is rather.

Col. H. Paints horribly.

Chas. P. Expect she does.

Col. H. In fact, an odious old creature. (Chas. P. *looks at him.*) Oh, don't be offended, and after all, it's charming Cecilia that you have in view. Miss Montagu can't help her mother being this or being that. I'll do my best for ye, my boy. (*Takes* Chas. P.'s *hand warmly and shakes it.*) I'll go to Russell Square to-morrow and open the campaign, and then I'll report progress. I've a letter to write, by-the-bye; you won't mind my running across to the hotel, and I'll join you at the breakfast-table in a quarter of an hour.   [*Exit to* R.

(*The voice of* Mr. Percival *is heard inside to* L.) Confound those military men, eating me out of house and home! That Colonel What's-his-name is always here. Cuss the Army! Bah! I've knocked my thumb for the fortieth time. (*Enters with a portmanteau in hand from* L.) Ah! (*greeting* Chas. P.)

CHAS. P. Ah! (*returns the salutation*).

MR. P. There's a van-load of things coming directly. I want to furnish that room upstairs as a study for myself. I'm going to read; it's a new idea, for which I'm rather obliged to Thingamee.

CHAS. P. (*aside*). Shouldn't have thought the article was so uncommon as that. (*Addressing his uncle.*) But you said, sir, that I was not to expect you till Friday, and I have told the Colonel that he can occupy the spare room.

MR. P. Eh?

CHAS. P. Of course, if I had expected you, I would have let him stop over the way.

MR. P. Ah! (*Throws his portmanteau on the table and rings the bell.*)

Enter SERVANT.

MR. P. Take the portmanteau up into my room, and let Colonel What's-his-name——

CHAS. P. Honeywood.

MR. P. Honeyman know that he can't have a bedroom here to-night, as Mr. Percival——

CHAS. P. But, please——

MR. P. I give information; I do not ask for it. Let James act on my instructions.

CHAS. P. This is my house, sir.

MR. P. But I pay the rent, sir.

CHAS. P, This is my servant, sir.

MR. P. Impertinence!

CHAS. P. As why? I merely repeat what you said yourself a moment ago. Why, you're spoilt, you know. There's your handsome sinecure, on which I could live like a prince, and look at what poetry brings me in! Next to nothing.

MR. P. (*contemptuously*). Ah!

CHAS. P. But it is an ennobling occupation. I delight in depicting the careers of our great dead in verse.

MR. P. Hang poetry! Hang the great dead! If you want to get your bread and cheese, which I take it you do (CHAS. P. *bows slightly*), I should advise you to look to the living and not to the dead. They speak of the "mighty spirits of the departed," but I could never see the point myself. I detest everything connected with literature down to goose, which is another name for quill-pens and indigestion.

CHAS. P. Ha, ha! Well, for a sort of dry humour, a kind of a laugh which would be a laugh if the salt-box hadn't been spilt over it, I never saw your match, sir.

MR. P. I'm very much out of sorts, and by no means in a humoristic vein (*pettishly*). This Miss What's-her-name——

CHAS. P. Montagu.

MR. P. Montagu,—seems to be a fair kind of

person, and what's more essential, she will probably have a good deal of money, which in your
case I take to be extremely desirable. You had
better see about it (*laughs drily*).

CHAS. P. (*calmly*). Would you wish me, sir, to
wait upon Mr. Montagu, and state to him, as a
man of business, that I intend, by his leave and
Mrs. Montagu's, to pay my addresses to Miss M.,
but that, meanwhile, in consequence of the de-
pressed condition of literature, I should be glad
of an advance of £20? (MR. P. *writhes a little,
and performs manœuvres indicative of inquietude.*)
Am I right in conjecturing that this is your view?
(MR. P. *paces the stage from* R. *to* L.)

MR. P. (*stopping short with his back turned to*
CHAS. P.). Ah, well, perhaps it wouldn't quite do.

CHAS. P. *Perhaps* not; but you've greater experience than I have. My own notion is, sir, I
frankly tell you, that the best way in these matters
is to cut a dash——

MR. P. (*aside*). Another cheque!

CHAS. P. (*continues*). For instance, I ought to
be able to present myself to the family of my
intended wife in suitable costume, and I cannot
very well order any fresh things of my tailor till
I have squared his account.

MR. P. How much may that be?

CHAS. P. (*pulls a bill out of his pocket*).

£56, 14s. 6d. (MR. P. *groans.*) Then one ought
to have proper supplies of boots, hats, gloves, and
so on.

MR. P. (*satirically*). Oh, yes, *and so on.* Is
there anything else, sir?

CHAS. P. Why, no gentleman wears the same
cravat (MR. P. *stares at him with increasing amazement*), or the same studs, or the same—in fact,
anything twice running.

MR. P. Oh, dear, no; *no gentleman* does, I'm
aware. *I* do; but that's another matter.

CHAS. P. I meant no disrespect to you, sir;
I merely intended to say that in my peculiar
situation it was necessary——

MR. P. To appear better off than you really
are—to let people suppose that you are a person
of independent property—which I wish were the
fact—and to favour the fallacious impression that
you have expectations from me!

CHAS. P. As you please, Oh, as you please, sir;
only I was going to observe, that supposing this is
to be done, a man can't visit such a house as the
Montagus' without making occasional presents.

MR. P. (*aside*). Ah!

CHAS. P. A box at the opera now and then——

MR. P. (*aside*). It's getting very late. (*Looks at
his watch.*)   Pheugh!

CHAS. P. (*pretending not to notice him*). A set

of emeralds given at the right moment has been known to clinch an affair of this kind.

MR. P. (*smiling ironically*). Has it? I don't think that I shall try the experiment.

CHAS. P. Then, to do the thing properly and carry matters with a high hand——

MR. P. (*aside*). Properly! With a high hand!

CHAS. P. One ought to lay on some sort of trap for the time.

MR. P. (*aside*). Good God!

CHAS. P. (*affecting unconsciousness*). If it was only an ordinary case, a gig or a drag might do; but where one plays for high stakes, there's no use in looking at a few pounds more or less——

MR. P. Oh, none at all!

CHAS. P. And I should recommend the regular thing.

MR. P. Perhaps you will have the goodness to explain, for my information, what you mean by *the regular thing?*

CHAS. P. Oh, a pair—a pair, of course. Powder isn't necessary, but——

MR. P. (*sarcastically*). Not while we're about it? You think it might possibly clinch, h—m?

CHAS. P. Of course, I don't mean to say that the thing couldn't be managed more economically (MR. P. *smiles and coughs*); but I was sketching out what struck me as the best road to success with Miss Montagu.

Mr. P. I see no harm in that.

Chas. P. Oh, my dear sir, you're too good!— I didn't expect——

Mr. P. (*drily*). No harm, I mean, in your sketching this out.

Chas. P. (*with a disconcerted air*). I misunderstood—I'm very sorry.

Mr. P. You appear to me to regard my resources as inexhaustible and as simply held in trust for you.

Chas. P. (*aside*). Hope they are! No such luck, I fear!

Mr. P. (*continues*). Now, I find (*takes out his banker's book and refers*) that I have let you have all that I intend to give you except £13, 19s. 3d. How far do you consider that that amount will go towards the accomplishment of the interesting programme you have just drawn up?

Chas. P. (*reckons*). Six times four and three-pence make precisely twenty-five shillings and sixpence; that's six pairs of gloves, which will last me three days. Frock-coat, five guineas: that makes seven pounds and sixpence. Carriage and pair and etceteras for week, six pounds eighteen shillings and ninepence: Total, £13, 19s. 3d. Wouldn't go very far, sir! (Mr. P. *gives a pro-*

*longed whistle, and retires up and leans out of the
window.* CHAS. P. *looks after him, shrugs his
shoulders, and then proceeds.*) I know what's in my
uncle's mind as well as if I was there listening.
He'll grumble and pay up. Not that I intend to
bleed him so extravagantly as I pretended just now,
not I. If Cecilia won't have me as I am, why
there's an end of it. Hang it! a man who has
been described in print as one of the four leading
poets of Great Britain, ahem! isn't to be despised.
I want money, and they want, ahem!—Well, it's
a fair exchange. The Colonel, besides, 'll be a
capital pioneer. Ah, here he comes.

Enter COLONEL HONEYWOOD *from* R.

COL. H. I'm almost ashamed of myself.

CHAS. P. Don't mention it, my dear Colonel.
Hope you have been attended to? Did you find
all you wanted?

COL. H. Breakfasted like a prince, dear boy—
like a prince. (MR. P. *turns round at window and
looks at the* COLONEL *through his spectacles.*) By-
the-bye, I thought you wouldn't mind me writing
a few letters, and asking your man to put stamps
on and let them go to the post?

CHAS. P. Of course not, of course not.

MR. P. (*aside*). Confounded effrontery!

COL. H. And, by-the-bye, I asked James to

B

lend me your portmanteau. (MR. P. *starts, but checks himself.*) He has taken it over to the Clarence for me. (CHAS. P. *looks rather serious.*) If you mind, you know, dear boy, I can send it back, but——

CHAS. P. Oh, no! oh, no! (*Aside.*) Cool! but it won't do, I s'ppose, to kick up a row.

COL. H. You don't happen to have any change about ye, dear boy? Off to Portsmouth to-night, and nothing about me but d—d country drafts. Back to-morrow on your business. We'll pull through there, dear boy; trust old Bob Honey-wood! Ah! you lucky dog!

CHAS. P. Well, Colonel, I'm rather short my-self, but if (*pulling a couple of sovereigns out of his pocket*) that'll do——

COL. H. Splendidly, dear boy, superbly. Re-turn them to-morrow.

CHAS. P. (*aside*). What a genial way he has!

MR. P. (*aside*). These military humbugs! I ought to look upon it as an honour, forsooth, to pay this person's travelling expenses down to Portsmouth. He'll go first class, no doubt; I always go second.

COL. H. Thankee, dear boy. Depend on me to-morrow. Hope I shall have to congratulate you and your esteemed parent (MR. P. *uses a gesture of disgust and resentment*). A man of high principle, but—(CHAS. P. *hushes him, puts his arm through his, and exeunt to* L. *both whispering and looking over their shoulders at* MR. P. *Exit* MR. P. *to* R. *looking over his shoulder at them*).

CURTAIN AND END OF ACT I.

ACT II.

SCENE I.

A boudoir in Russell Square. MRS. *and* MISS
    MONTAGU. *The latter is at the piano and
    sings.* MISS MONTAGU'S *maid is seated at
    the window* R. *side embroidering.*

> A fair girl sat by a leafless tree :
> Her cheek on her hand was pillowed :
> And all that I heard was, "Woe is me !
>   My love is dead !"

MISS M. (*rising and sitting by* MRS. M.) Ah,
well, that is enough. I really think, my dearest
mother, that Uncle Ralph might be more consider-
ate than to teaze us with so many letters of introduction. He is so terribly anxious to get me married,
that he no sooner meets with some notability or
other on the Continent, than he despatches him
post-haste to Russell Square, Bloomsbury, with a
passport to us, just to see whether he will do.

MRS. M. (*who is rather deaf, imposing her hands,
as if in the act of benediction*) My darling Cecilia !

MISS M. It is really becoming dreadful. I

am sure that I shall end by doing something which will create an immense sensation—throw myself into the Regent's Canal or marry a corporal in the Grenadiers.

MRS. M. My darling Cecilia! (*deprecatingly, with the arms imposed as before*).

MISS M. (*mischievously*). Mrs. Corporal Smith! I am sure it would sound highly respectable.

MAID. Oh! Miss, don't talk so horridly.

MISS M. Horridly? Why, what can be worse than Mrs. Bread-and-Butter? (*The others look inquiringly*, MRS. M. *assuming an air of bland benevolence.*) Yes, to be sure, that Mynheer Butterbrode, who is one of the desirable alliances thrown in my way by my Uncle Ralph—his name is Dutch for bread-and-butter.

MAID (*aside*). He looks to me as if *he* was Dutch for bread-and-butter!

MISS M. (*aside*, MRS. M. *looking on with an air of imperturbable serenity, but only catching a word here and there*) Then my beloved parent is so deaf unhappily, and papa is engaged all day at the Bank, so that it falls upon me to receive these distinguished persons, to ask them who they are, what they want, whether they are respectable, whether they are rich enough to keep a wife—of course all in a most roundabout and genteel manner; for I would not give Uncle Ralph's friends offence for the world.

Mrs. M. (*with unlimited benignity*). My darling
Cecilia, no offence, I am sure. (Miss M. *bows
acquiescence.*)

Miss M. (*aside*). Poor dear!—It's a sort of
march past, and I am expected to select the fortunate candidate.   Uncle Ralph's ideas of a
suitable match for a girl with no inconsiderable
prospects must be rather singular.   I declare I
could have found it in my heart to box his ears
the other day, if he had been within reach, when
he sent that frightful Prince Pippinhoff with a
letter assuring papa that all Vienna was in love
with him, and that, if some mines of his turned
out well, he would be the richest man in Austria.
What did you say, Jeannette?

Jeann. Oh, nothing, Miss. (*Aside.*) All I know
is, I saw him borrow two pounds of master the
other night when he dined here—to carry on those
mines, I shouldn't wonder.   If some people are
not credolous!   (*To* Miss M.) Oh, Miss, I see
Colonel Honeywood coming up the other side of
the square, and he has just crossed over, as if he
was coming here, Miss.

Miss M. Colonel Honeywood, mother.

Mrs. M. (*rising with tranquil deliberation*). Delighted, my dear Col——

Miss M. (*laughing*). No, no; not yet.   I said
he was coming.   Jeannette sees him in the square.

(MRS. M. *imposes hands on* MISS M. *and* JEAN-NETTE *and resumes her seat.*) I cannot quite make him out. Not that he often presents himself here, and when he does, it generally turns out that there is some object. (MISS M. *retires up, and reclines on sofa.*)

Enter SERVANT.

SERV. (*to* MRS M., *who smiles benignly, but does not appear to hear*). Colonel Honeywood, madam. He wishes to know if it will be convenient for you to see him?

MISS M. Ask the Colonel to come up. Mamma does not hear. [*Exit* SERV.

Enter COLONEL HONEYWOOD *from* R.

COL. H. (*springing forward to* L., *where* MRS. M. *has risen to receive him*). It is always, my dearest madam, one of the greatest pleasures of my life to see you in the enjoyment of your usual health and spirits. I hope (*turns round slightly*)—but I see that Miss Montagu is present. Double pleasure! (*Goes up to sofa, and is met by* MISS M.) My dear Miss Montagu, I am charmed to see you looking so well—charmed.

MISS M. You are a perfect stranger, Colonel; it seems an age since you were here. You remind me of the comets. (MRS. M. *retires to window and converses with* JEANNETTE.)

COL. H. My dear Miss Montagu, I bring with me a *tale*, which I trust will not be so powerful for evil as the *tails* of the comets are sometimes said to be.

MISS M. Nor so long, Colonel, eh! But, to be serious, what tale do you refer to. A tale of knight-errantry perhaps?

COL. H. Well, I am doing an errand for a friend, but I do it in the morning; therefore mine may be called a tale of *morning-errandry*. (*Aside.*) I meant that for a joke, but I see she does not take it. Well, well!

MISS M. You're still mysterious, Colonel. Who, then, is your friend? Do you expect me to draw you out?

COL. H. Briefly, the matter stands thus——

Enter SERVANT.

SERV. (*to* MRS. M.) The Prince Rhodomontados waits below, madam.

MRS. M. (*returning to her seat*) Let the Prince be asked up. My darling Cecilia!

MISS M. (*affecting surprise*) Yes, my dearest mother.

MRS. M. (*with slight warmth*) His Highness, child.

MISS M. Very well, my dearest mother. (*Aside.*) This is the Athenian hero, Prince Themistocles

Rhodomontados, who presented his credentials lately to papa from Uncle Ralph. How absurd to think that I should ever marry such a man! He scarcely knows a word of English, and I scarcely know a word of Greek, except *hic, hæc, hoc.*

COL. H. Well, another time I may hope to have the pleasure—(*Draws designs on the carpet with his cane, and prepares to take leave.*) (*Aside.*) Most opportune, by Jove! I was beginning at the wrong end. That deaf old woman put my ideas all out of my head. People oughtn't to be so deaf. (*To* MRS. M.) My dearest madam, just one moment. Have you seen the Percivals lately?

MRS. M. (*with matchless suavity, but unconscious of the Colonel's question*) My dear Colonel!

MISS M. Mamma does not quite catch what you said, Colonel Honeywood. She was saying only the other day, that she wondered Charles or his uncle had not been here.

COL. H. (*agreeably*). Rather odd sort of people? —I speak under correction—I have heard as much.

MISS M. The uncle—yes. But Charles is a fine, open-hearted, frank fellow.

COL. H. Doubtless; like all the young, he's fond of society, partial to spending money—(*aside*) when he can get any,—a leetle gay, like most of us before we sober down.

MRS. M. But you do not mean to say, my dearest Colonel——

COL. H. Oh, no, by no means, madam. I never cast imputations. Oh, yes, Charlie—I call him Charlie—I was his father's friend (*brushes his eye*)—is an excellent chap, and frank, as you say, frank—to a fault! We happened the other day to be speaking of you. He said he wished there was more sincerity in the world—less humbug, in fact, was his phrase.

MRS. M. But you do not mean——

COL. H. Dear, dear, no, madam. I hate detractors above everything. I would not take away a man's character for the world. I was merely giving an instance of his candour. He also said, I remember, that it was perfectly ridiculous to see how some old ladies of one's acquaintance tried to make themselves look young.

MRS. M. But I hope, my dear sir——

COL. H. I assure you, my dear madam, I have the greatest detestation of personalities. Ah! and he happened—I merely mention it *en passant* as an illustration of his fine open character—(MRS. M. *bows;* MISS M. *averts her head as if in displeasure*)—that it was a pity to see ladies who were old enough to be grandmammas putting on juvenile airs.

MRS. M. But, my dear Colonel——

COL. H. Of course not, my dear Mrs. Montagu. I have the strongest dislike to tittle-tattle and scandal.

MRS. M. (*imposes her hands, but* MISS M. *smiles satirically aside.* COL. H. *retires up, and looks out of window, slipping something on the way into* JEANNETTE'S *hand.*) Ah! I see it doesn't rain. (*Bows to ladies, moves over to* L. *and exit.*)

JEANN. (*aside*). There's something very superior in these officers. A fiver! Young Percival never gave me a shilling in his life. Don't believe myself he was a University man. (MRS. *and* MISS M. *converse in an undertone.*)

Enter SERVANT, *ushering in the* PRINCE RHODOMONTADOS *from* R.

SERV. His Highness the Prince.

MRS. M. (*advancing*). Prince, this is too great an honour!

MISS M. (*somewhat distantly*) I trust your Highness is well. (*Aside.*) How much better I love the good English faces!

PR. R. (*in broken English*). I am sharmed, mesdames. Madame Montagu, your omble sarvant. Mademoiselle Montagu, your omble sarvant. I called at you for to sartify that my bohx at opera is wacant this efening, and is at your total disposition. If you shall go, I vill be entranced.

MRS. M. My dear Prince, you are too good. (*Imposes hands on the* PRINCE.)

MISS M. (*aside*). Oh, deliver me from these foreign invaders! (*To* PR. R.) How delightful!

PR. R. Veatter jolly fine; almost, I think, too jolly fine. I eat strawberry other day, and he give me stomach-ache! (MRS. M. *and* MISS M. *use deprecatory gestures.*) Vish you joy, mesdames, of your bohx, and make you sure of my distinguished consideration. *Bon jour.*   [*Exit.*

MISS M. These foreign gentlemen are strangely distasteful to me, my dearest mother, and father and Uncle Ralph have such an opinion of them! (*Aside.*) That Colonel Honeywood—I don't know why I should suspect it, but I do—was trying to prejudice mamma against Charles Percival. There's something about the Colonel which I don't like. I wonder what it can be?

MRS. M. We have lived longer in the world than you have, child, and know better what is for your happiness. You have unlimited opportunities; wealth and rank are at your feet. If you do not admire the Prince Rhodomontados, my dear——

MISS M. (*aside*). That I certainly don't.

MRS. M. Or Mynheer Butterbrode——

MISS M. (*aside*). The horror!

MRS. M. Why, there is the Earl of Ambleside, young, handsome, and accomplished; and has not your Uncle Ralph promised to get him made a Duke and a Knight of the Garter, if you will have him?

Miss M. And is not Charles handsome and accomplished too, my dearest mother?

Mrs. M. Charles?

Miss M. Charles Percival, to be sure. You know whom I mean, mother, don't you?

Mrs. M. Charles Percival, Cecilia, is certainly young; whether he is handsome, is a matter of taste; whether he is accomplished, I am not competent to decide; but he is not an Earl, and— in short, your father and myself look upon the connection as objectionable. Those very poor persons are never desirable, my dear; they have always a something about them.

Miss M. But I never understood that the Percivals were so *very* poor, my dearest mother; and besides, why could not uncle have Charles *made an Earl*, then a Marquis, finally a Duke and K.G.? It is so easy now.

Mrs. M. A couple of penniless adventurers baiting a trap for an heiress, my darling Cecilia. (*Aside.*) That young Percival must be a very illbred and impertinent fellow. The Colonel has quite opened my eyes.

Miss M. Old Mr. Percival is certainly a little eccentric——

MRS. M. Very much so, my dear—viciously so. People in their humble circumstances have no right to be eccentric.

MISS M. At any rate, Charles is not. (*Aside.*) That wicked Colonel! How I scorn a back-biter!

MRS. M. I have less confidence in his principles than I could wish. You had better turn this matter over seriously, my dearest; but I should recommend you to give up all idea of the Percivals. The alliance shall never have my approbation, and I think you are acquainted with your father's views. Let us drop the subject for the present. It is almost time to dress for dinner.   [*Exit.*

JEANN. (*advancing from window*). You look pale, Miss, this afternoon! You are not ill? Let me get a chair.

MISS M. (*laying a hand on her arm*). Oh, no, it will be over presently; merely a passing faintness. The sultry weather, I dare say. There, it's gone. (*Brightens up.*) Look here, Jeannette.

JEANN. Yes, Miss.

MISS M. Listen to me, Jeannette.

JEANN. I do, Miss.

MISS M. But listen to me, Jeannette.

JEANN. I am all attention, Miss.

MISS M. Well, now, Jeannette, tell me, what do you think of the Prince?

JEANN. Oh, Miss, it's not my place to offer an opinion.

MISS M. When I call upon you, Jeannette, it is.

JEANN. Well, Miss, I should say he hadn't had the best masters. (MISS M. *smiles*.) He's better than Mynheer Butterbrode, though; or than that Herr Schmidt. But oh, Miss, Colonel Honeywood for me!

MISS M. For *you*, Jeannette?

JEANN. For *you*, Miss, I meant. No, he's too old for *me*. He might be my—papa, Miss.

MISS M. (*smiling*). A very proper objection, Jeannette. But Colonel Honeywood is not a foreigner, you silly!

JEANN. (*consideringly*). No? But he has served in foreign parts, Miss.

MISS M. He has your good opinion, I see, at any rate. Mamma is not very well, I think, to-day.

JEANN. (*archly*) She talked very crossly about Mr. Charles, Miss, I thought. Now, if the Colonel wasn't in the case, I should have said that Mr. Charles——

MISS M. (*sharply*) The Colonel in the case? Who ever authorised you to suppose that he *was* in the case?

JEANN. No offence, I hope, Miss. Really, it seemed to me——

MISS M. Yes, I'm vexed with you, but never

mind; there, don't cry—(JEANNETTE *puts her hand-kerchief to her face and sobs*)—there, it's all forgotten (*soothingly*). I don't know what has come to you, Jeannette. (*Aside.*) It seems as if everybody was turning against us. I wish Charles would write some great poem that would create a furor. I will tell him to. I declare I never thought of it before. Then, again, I wish that old uncle of his wouldn't be so absurd, but would learn to behave himself like other people. (*To* JEANNETTE.) Come, come, Jeannette, and help me to dress for dinner. Oh ! (*she screams.*)

JEANN. Oh ! (*screams.*)

CHARLES PERCIVAL *springs in at the window.*

CHAS. P. Hush ! for goodness-sake. Be still as mice, both of you.

MISS M. Oh, Charles !

CHAS. P. I climbed up by the water-pipe and the trellis-work, and broke my arm as near as a toucher against the window-ledge. But never mind. Jeannette, lock the door, and don't say a word ; that's a brick. (JEANNETTE *looks at her mistress and hesitates;* CHAS. P. *hastens to the door and secures it himself.*) There ! I've not a moment to lose, Cecilia. (*He speaks in a hurried undertone.* JEANNETTE *has retired up a little, and looks from one to the other in amazement.*) I have a scheme in my head. I am off to Rotterdam by the next steamer. I shall see your Uncle Ralph. I shall explain to him how matters stand. He was always very civil to me, you know, Cecilia, and does not think me such a bad fellow——

Miss M. Such a bad fellow, Charles!

Jeann. I think I hear a footstep. I think I hear two.

Miss M. Heavens! Charles, for pity's sake, go. But how will you go? There is only that door.

Chas. P. Go? *Viâ* water-pipe and trellis, to be sure. If your uncle is favourable, I shall form some plan in concert with him; if he is unfavourable——

Miss M. What then, Charles?

Chas. P. I shall go to America, and try to forget that I ever loved a rich man's daughter.

Miss M. (*reproachfully*) Oh, cruel, cruel! If any one should come! (*She joins her hands in terror.*)

Jeann. I'm sure there's somebody; it is a man's tread. (*Puts her ear to the keyhole.*)

Chas. P. Cecilia, I did not mean that; I was mad when I said it. I meant that I should endeavour to overcome my presumptuous passion for one so much above me. God bless you! (*Kisses her, while* Jeannette *is intent on the door.*) I shall be back

c

in three or four days. (*Hastens to the window ; it has grown darker ; the sound of footsteps on the stairs becomes more distinct ;* MISS M. *follows him to the window.*) Now for it ! By Jove! no such easy matter. There ! (*Gets a footing on the trellis, and half disappears ; a tap comes at the door.*)

JEANN. What is it?

MRS. M. (*without*). Let me in instantly.

MISS M. (*making a gesture to* JEANNETTE) Why don't you open the door to mamma? Have you hampered the lock ? (*Looks down to see if* CHAS. P. *has alighted safely, and makes a sign to* JEANNETTE *to open the door.*)

CHAS. P. (*from below*). God bless you ! See you again soon. Hope for good news.

Enter MRS. MONTAGU *hurriedly.*

MRS. M. Whose voice was that? A man's? .

JEANN. Perhaps mine, ma'am ; I'm a little hoarse to-day (*coughs*).

MISS M. I was a little faint, and thought the air might do me good. Perhaps it was a man in the street whom you heard, my dearest mother. In our noisy neighbourhood, it is difficult to account for every sound ; is it not, Jeannette?

JEANN. (*hoarsely*). Very, Miss.

MRS. M. (*imposing her hand*). I suppose it was a mistake of mine, my dear Cecilia. You will keep everybody waiting, if you do not prepare for dinner, child. Come. [*Exit.*

MISS M. (*aside to* JEANN.) Run to the street door, and see if you can distinguish anything of Mr. Charles, Jeannette. If anything were to happen to him while he is away—God forbid!—I should love you all the better, Jeannette, for being the last who saw him. I must follow my mother. [*Exit.*

JEANN. (*aside*). How heavy that five-pound note I had from the Colonel lies on my conscience! I think, if I ever become a rich woman, and could do without it, I will give it to the poor. My young mistress is a bit crazy about young Percival, and perhaps it would not be wise for me to stand out too much for the Colonel. Time may bring the young man to a sense of his duty; at any rate, I'll give him one more chance. [*Exit.*

SCENE 2.

Manager's parlour at the Bank of MONTAGU BROTHERS, *Lombard Street.* MR. CECIL MONTAGU, *the head of the firm, discovered in consultation with his head-clerk. He is seated at a table covered with papers; the clerk stands.*

MR. M. Well, Travers, I think we must break off for to-day. I have to be home early. Good-day to ye—good-day. I hope Mrs. Travers and the children are quite well?

T. Thankee, sir, quite well. That eldest boy of mine——

Mr. M. I'm very glad to hear it—good-bye.

[*Exit* Travers.

Mr. M. (*solus*). He's a very worthy fellow, but he is unfortunately one of those men who have got an eldest boy, and keep him constantly in ambush, ready to spring out at one like a Jack-in-the-box. The worst of it is, if you give the youngster a desk, you don't get rid of the affair, for the gap is filled up like clockwork by the eldest boy *at home*. Travers has twelve boys— a somewhat alarming prospect. I think I must recommend a colonial career for some of them, get him to recruit the Line with a few, to send a careful selection to sea, and so on. Well, well, time will show, and just now, to say the truth, I have my own little troubles, or rather my one great trouble—the settlement of my girl somehow. If I was a poor man—my brother Ralph and I were poor enough when we began life, God knows!—there'd have been no difficulty. I should have looked for some honest young fellow with a clear head and a pair of strong arms, and if Cecilia and he loved each other, he should have had her, with my blessing—all, perhaps, that I should have had to give. But, as we bankers say, circumstances alter cases. Cecilia was always a most dutiful child, and I have often heard her say that it would cut her to the very heart to contradict her mother or me, or run counter to our wishes. Yet the little gipsy, to my knowledge, has been her own mistress ever since she left off pinafores; does exactly as she pleases, and what is more, makes us do exactly as she pleases. But, as we bankers say, a line must be drawn somewhere; and Mrs. M. and myself strongly object to this proposed alliance with young Percival. The young fellow himself would be all very well, but he has an intractable oddity in the shape of an uncle, who has hitherto defied with complete success all our attempts to make head or tail of him. It is by all accounts a singular household; they appear to have no relations; they see no company; Charles has no profession and no means. I am sorry for the poor fellow, who has plenty of natural talent and engaging manners; but his father—a most worthy man, without a particle of this unfortunate eccentricity—died when he was very young—a mere child. Soon afterwards he lost his mother, and my brother Ralph, who had known the family in our humble days, when he was glad enough to be asked to the Percivals on Sundays, felt an interest in the little orphan, and offered to bring him up. But this uncle, the same with whom Charles still lives, objected, threw difficulties in the way, and the proposition of the banker's clerk (my brother was at that time nothing more) was somewhat rudely, as I have always understood, rejected. Yet, for the sake of old associations, Ralph, a soft-hearted fellow—he and I might have stood quite at the top of the tree, I have told him over and over again, if we had not done in our time so many rash acts of generosity—Ralph, I say, kept up the acquaintance of these Percivals, uncle and nephew, and when he went out to Rotterdam to establish a branch of our house there, recommended them to us as people of whom it was his express desire that we should see as much as possible. Why? Because, for-sooth, of those Sunday-dinners he ate at Charles's father's, when they were well-to-do sort of folks, and he was a poor and struggling man; and he has said to me over and over again: "Cecil, the Percivals must never want while Montagu Brothers have a sovereign in the till, for you and I have dined at Mr. Percival's *when we had hardly the money in our pockets to buy a meal elsewhere.*" Well, so it was that Charles came to be intimate at our house, and that Cecilia and he knew each other as boy and girl. Heigho! I have come round to the opinion, some time ago, that we men of business are shrewd fellows in our counting-houses and fools by our own firesides. To think that I, with all my practical experience and knowledge of the world, should have been blind to the wide disproportion which years would create between the circumstances of the two! that I should not have foreseen, till it was almost too late, what an unwise policy it was not to sever the kind of romantic tie before it grew too strong and rooted itself too deeply. My wife was right. Women, I have observed, are generally very right—or very wrong. How often she has warned me! But I was proof against all she could say, because I feared that Ralph would take it unkindly, and because—well, Cecilia was not indifferent to him. Then, when my brother at last perceived that some serious disadvantages might arise from the connection— mere money was not in his thoughts, but Henry Percival the uncle's strange ways, and poor Charles's want of *status*—the mischief was done ; Cecilia had grown up into womanhood, and instead of the child's love she had had for Percival, we could very well see there was the woman's love. We encouraged other suitors, and tried to discountenance Charles's visits; but it *was* of little use. Our thought was that she might find a suitable home, where, in the society of a husband

worthy—well, why should I not say of her good
fortune?—she would forget gradually this youthful
fancy, this passion of her girlhood.   But no! She's
as hard to move as an Ecclesiastical Commission,
and has as many reasons at her back as a Spanish
Jesuit——

Re-enter TRAVERS.

T. Young Mr. Percival is in the outer office,
sir, and wishes to see you, if convenient.

MR. M. Eh? eh? who? (*Rises and paces* R.
to L.)   Deuced awkward!   What does he want?

T. I don't know, sir.

MR. M. Hang it, man! what does he *look* as
if he wanted?

T. (*smiling*). I am no physiognomist, sir, and
really cannot tell.

MR. M. D'ye think it'd do to tell him I can't
see him?

T. Very great friend of Mr. Ralph's, sir.

MR. M. What the devil do you mean, sir, by
telling me that? as if I didn't know it.   (*Aside.*)
That's just where it is.   I suppose I must see him.
Perhaps he is short of money, poor fellow!   (*To*
TRAVERS.)   Does he look as if—as if—he was——

T. No, sir, I don't think he does.   He's not
dressed well enough for *that*.   I think, sir, if it
was *that*, he'd have taken more pains with himself.
I have noticed, in the course of my forty years'

experience, that the happiest faces and the nappiest coats—(*checks himself on seeing that* MR. M. *has a remarkably cheerful expression and a very new coat*).

MR. M. Yes!

T. I was going to say, sir, were not invariably——

MR. M. Just so! We must not keep Mr. Percival waiting—ask him to step in to me.

T. Very good, sir. (*Aside.*) Poor Mr. Charles looks terribly disconsolate. I'd lay an odd thousand he's had a tiff with Miss Cecilia. I saw her pass up the street just this moment, walking as if she had been a mere common lady, and as grave as a goose in the rain. There's something in the wind; hope it isn't a double murder and suicide, because that'll be bad for the reputation of the Bank.

MR. M. (*who has resumed his seat, looking up*). What! haven't you——

T. Going, sir.   [*Exit.*

Enter CHARLES PERCIVAL, *very quietly dressed in morning costume. He appears to be in low spirits. They exchange bows, and then shake hands.*

MR. M. (*rather coolly*). It is not often that I have this pleasure, Charles. I conclude that some little matter of business——

CHAS. P. Y—y-es, it was some—little matter of —business, Mr. Montagu. Perhaps, I ought rather to have said—a—*great* matter of—business— hem!

MR. M. A great matter—of—business? Hem! hem!

CHAS. P. Hem! hem! (*He plays with the rim of his hat and seems at a loss how to begin.*)

MR. M. (*rubbing his hands with assumed geniality and cheerfulness*). Not any little money affair. Always most delighted——

CHAS. P. (*with forced gaiety*) Oh, no; oh, dear, dear, no, my dear sir. I assure you——

MR. M. (*in a good-natured tone, but still formal*). I'm pleased to find it is so. I only thought that there might be something of the sort, and that you might have a delicacy——

CHAS. P. (*who still stands with one hand resting on the table*). No; the fact is, Mr. Montagu, I came to you to-day on a very different and, as I conceive, a much more important, errand. (MR. M. *coughs.*) I—that is, I mean, your daughter Cecilia—that is—(MR. M. *looks up with a sarcastic expression on his countenance.*) There is an attach- ment, Mr. Montagu, of old standing between us.

MR. M. (*distantly*). I am aware of it, sir, and you, I believe, as well as the lady, are aware of my sentiments in regard to it.

CHAS. P. But might not those sentiments be changed by circumstances?

MR. M. They might, I allow; but where are the circumstances? I beg that you will be seated, however; pray, excuse——

CHAS. P. (*with scarcely perceptible irony*) Oh, thank ·you very much, I'm sure, for being so thoughtful. (*They both bring chairs to the front.*) Well, the circumstances are these. With my uncle's concurrence and help—(MR. M. *arches his eyebrows very slightly*) — I propose at once to seek a partnership in a wealthy concern. If I succeed, of which I have every expectation, I should at once secure position and means; I should no longer be what I have been, what I *am*—a person without a calling and without a shilling of my own. I should feel myself worthier of Miss Montagu; I should feel that I was not asking her and you, and Mrs. Montagu, to make so great a sacrifice either for her sake or for mine. I should feel that I had something more than my heart to offer her; and though I could not make her a princess, Mr. Montagu, I would try hard to make her happy—happier than she is.

MR. M. (*calmly*) It is your opinion, I am to infer, that at present my daughter is not happy?

CHAS. P. It is.

MR. M. Then, sir, what I say is, damn your

opinion. (CHAS. P. *starts and draws his chair
back*.) (*Aside*.) Dare say he's not far wrong. (*To*
CHAS. P., *satirically*.) Pray, sir, is this opinion of
yours professional or unprofessional?

CHAS. P. Unprofessional, Mr. Montagu, and, if
you please, worthless.

MR. M. Thank you. Did you not speak just
now of a partnership, a-hem?

CHAS. P. I did.

MR. M. In a wealthy concern, a-hem?

CHAS. P. Yes.

MR. M. In this country, a-hem?

CHAS. P. Abroad.

MR. M. Partnerships in wealthy concerns are
not very easily procured, I believe. Are they,
Mr. Percival?

CHAS. P. You ought to be a better judge, sir,
than myself. But not to detain you unnecessarily,
the object of my visit is to ascertain from you
whether, in the event of my attainment of a share
in this house, which I am not at liberty to name
at present (MR. M. *bows assent*), you will consent
to our union?

MR. M. I may say at once, certainly not.

CHAS. P. Then, Mr. Montagu, our interview
may be considered at an end (*rises as if to take
leave*). I quite counted on your readiness to re-
consider——

Mr. M. That is a different question.

Chas. P. (*with ill-disguised eagerness*) That is all I ask.

Mr. M. Have you any means of forming an approximate idea of your prospects under these new auspices?

Chas. P. The business is said to be worth £400,000 a year, with an invested capital of six millions. (Mr. M. *opens his eyes, and squares round in his chair to* Chas. P., *who smiles faintly*.)

Mr. M. Are you aware, Mr. Charles, that the figures you give represent rather more, if anything, than the assets of the Bank of Montagu Brothers? We would not give a man a partnership in our house if he were to offer to lay down £500,000.

Chas. P. (*placidly*) I hope, Mr. Montagu, by a little favour, to obtain what I seek for a somewhat smaller consideration—somewhat smaller. (*Aside*.) *Very much* smaller.

Mr. M. In a very large way, of course.

Chas. P. Yes. A leading banking-house. Your line, you see. (*Looks at* Mr. M. *with an air of complacency*.) Cecilia would feel thoroughly at home, my dear sir.

Mr. M. (*rather mystified*) In-deed! A ban—ban——

Chas. P. Banking-house, yes. £400,000 a

year, with six millions of invested capital! What do you say, sir?

MR. M. £400,000 a year, with six millions of invested capital, is, a-hem! a very good thing. The house of Montagu, Charles, was half-a-century building up such a fortune, and all I can tell you is, that if you can step into the same ready-made, you may consider yourself a devilish lucky fellow.

CHAS. P. You are incredulous, Mr. Montagu?

MR. M. (*deliberately*) I *am*, Mr. Percival. (*Rises as if desirous of terminating the interview.*)

CHAS. P. But one word more. I appeal to you, sir (MR. M. *inclines his head slightly*). All I demand—at least, solicit, I would say—at your hands is this: to promise me that, if within a month from the present time, I am prepared to lay before you the deed of partnership, you will withdraw your opposition to my wishes.

MR. M. (*after a pause*) I may say that on those terms I consent. But understand distinctly: I pledge myself *alone*. (*Gets his hat down from the rail, and begins to brush it with his sleeve.*) Myself alone.

CHAS. P. Accept my very best thanks, Mr. Montagu. I will observe the condition you have imposed on me; but let me now impose a condition on you, that is, that you will regard this conversation as strictly private?

MR. M. On all accounts I am willing to do so. My train leaves for Streatham in a quarter of an hour; you must excuse me.

CHAS. P. (*moving off*) Good-bye. (*Aside.*) So far, so good. [*Exit to* R.

MR. M. (*moving off and aside*) If that young man doesn't tell a different tale when we next come across each other, I'm strangely mistaken. Some practical joker at the bottom of it, I suspect. (*Claps on his hat and hurries out to* L.)

CURTAIN.

SCENE 3.

Morning-room at MR. PERCIVAL'S. *Room discovered with luggage scattered about the floor, on the chairs, &c.* SERVANT *discovered brushing clothes busily.*

SERV. They say that listeners never hear any good of themselves. What if they don't? They hear plenty of bad about other people, which makes up for it. Besides, I like to listen. It gives one an insight into human nature. One gets a knowledge of character. Without listening life would be a burden. As if a man could live on brushing clothes and handing potatoes, reading

the newspaper and looking in the glass, shaving a
man who is as smooth as a teacup, and being
called a d—d fool a hundred times a day for
twenty pounds a year without extras.   Listening's
my only perquisite ; it is the working-man's friend,
the slave's luxury.   I heard the other day (*lowers
his voice and puts his hand to his mouth*) a tre-
mendous secret.   Old master, in an uncontrollable
impulse of romantic generosity, has given young
master a ten-pound note for the purpose of
enabling young master to establish himself in a
wealthy concern, which is worth eight hundred
million a year and twenty thousand of invested
capital !   I'd give something for a draught of good
ale after that ; it makes a poor man wonderful dry
to have such mythological figures passing through
his mouth ; they lap up all the moisture as they
go.   I heard old master say to young master, too,
that ten pounds was ten pounds, which I think
old master must have caught from some sharp
chap or other on 'Change, or else 'tis his natural
talent.   Well, young master's off to the Continent
to-morrow, and is perfectly wild with excitement.
" Oh," says he, " never mind the money.   Brush my
blue suit ; buy me a one-and-sixpenny travelling-
cap, and take my passage in the Rotterdam boat,
fore-cabin."   In fact, young master has become
quite an altered man within these last few days ;

and I have always observed that, when these metamorphoses take place (*lowers his voice, and puts his hand to his mouth, looking round him*) a *woman's* in the case. (CHAS. P. *enters unperceived.*) Ha! ha! Mr. Charles, I see what your little game——

CHAS. P. (*confronting him suddenly*). What the devil do you mean, sir?

SERV. (*terrified out of his wits*). Ho! dear me, sir, how you frightened me! I was just going to say——

CHAS. P. Hold your tongue, sir, and don't tell me any of your damned lies. Luggage not ready yet? What, in the name of Beelzebub, have you been doing all the morning? (*Passes* R. *to* L. *and* L. *to* R. *in a state of irritable excitement.*) Idle hound! useless incumbrance! (SERV. *recedes up, as* CHAS. P. *throws his arms about and makes as if he was going to strike him.*) Infernal blockhead! (*Throws a carpet-bag at* SERV., *who darts through the open window.*) I'm distracted! my brain swims! I feel already as if this great venture of mine was turning my head. But I must go through with it. Neck or nought. It is a question of life or death. I haven't a moment to lose. I had a hurried note last night from Cecilia to say that the Colonel is gaining ground fast with her mother; that she detests the man, but that extra-

ordinary pressure is being put upon her. My
father's friend indeed! Hypocrite! He infatuates
the old woman, Cecilia says, with his attentions,
and his big talk about his immense possessions
in the West Indies (a paltry falsehood!), and his
doings in the Punjaub, and his family, in which
he has induced her to believe there is a dormant
barony! She actually snubbed the Greek prince,
it seems, and the Dutch burgomaster, when they
came the other day. So much the better! As for
the Colonel, now that he has seriously entered the
field and got Mrs. Montagu's ear, he's a more for-
midable rival, but I'll be a match for him yet.

[*Exit to* L.

Enter MR. PERCIVAL *from* R.

MR. P. (*nearly stumbling over a portmanteau*)
Good God! what's the meaning of this? My
dining-room turned into a luggage-van! I was
expecting to find lunch on the table, and instead
I see nothing but a hat-box and a railway-rug.
I'm hanged if they're not my hat-box and my
railway-rug! (*Turns over the various things.*) Why,
the impudent young dog has appropriated my
best portmanteau! And my patent what-dye-call-
it! And my last new umbrella! This is more
than I can bear. (*Rings the bell and begins to pace
the room.*)

Enter SERVANT.

SERV. (*aside*). I see what's coming! No joke to be baited alive by wild masters like this for twenty pounds a year and no livery!

MR. P. Get these things out of the way forthwith and lay luncheon. Whoever saw such an infernal confusion?

SERV. It was Mr. Charles's express order that they should remain here, sir.

MR. P. And it's *my* express order, sir, that they may be removed instantly.

SERV. (*with an air of perplexity*). Mr. Charles told me it was as much as my place was worth to touch anything.

MR. P. (*peremptorily*). And I tell you, sir, that it is as much as your place is worth to leave anything here. Take them away—take them away. (*Kicks the luggage about.*)

SERV. (*in an agony of despair*). Mr. Charles will give me notice if I do.

MR. P. And I will give you notice if you don't.

[SERVANT *in a phrenzy snatches up port-manteau, throws it over his shoulder, and is going out to* R. *when he runs over* CHARLES PERCIVAL *entering.*

CHAS. P. What the dickens are you about? I thought I told you—(*sees his uncle, who has retired up.*) Ah!

MR. P. Ah!

CHAS. P. Thought you had gone to East-bourne.

MR. P. Imagined you were off to Rotterdam. (*Servant profits by opportunity and exit.*)

CHAS. P. But I suppose you're going?

MR. P. Not till the morning. I suppose *you* are?

CHAS. P. Not till the morning.

MR. P. (*muttering aside*). Damn!

CHAS. P. (*muttering aside*). Damn!

MR. P. But I have asked Humphreys to occupy the spare room to-night, fancying it would be vacant! He was particularly anxious to see me before I went to Eastbourne.

CHAS. P. Most singular coincidence! I have asked Harrison to occupy the spare room to-night, fancying it would be vacant! He had a special desire to say good-bye before I left for Holland.

MR. P. Well, all I can suggest is that Harrison should get a bed at the Clarence.

CHAS. P. I was just about to remark that Humphreys had better secure a bed at the George.

MR. P. Ah, bah! I know Humphreys too well to dream of offering him such a slight.

CHAS. P. My intimacy with Harrison enables me, my dear sir, to state most confidently that knocking him down would be a trifle compared to making him such a proposal.

MR. P. I shall be very glad to see this affair of yours settled.

CHAS. P. (*aside*). So shall I, by Jove.

MR. P. Then I suppose I shall have to sleep at the Clarence to accommodate Harrison!

CHAS. P. And I suppose I shall have to go to the George to make room for Humphreys!

MR. P. (*between his teeth*). Damn!   [*Exit.*

CHAS. P. (*quickly*) Hang it, what a bore!
                                        [*Exit.*

CURTAIN.   END OF ACT II.

ACT III.

SCENE I.

Drawing-room at the MONTAGUS' *as before ;* MISS
MONTAGU *and* COLONEL HONEYWOOD *discovered at the piano ;* MRS. MONTAGU *at window.*

MISS MONTAGU *sings.*

*Hence, all you vain delights,
As short as are the nights
Wherein you spend your folly !
There's naught in this life sweet,
If men were wise to see't,
But only melancholy,
Oh, sweetest melancholy !*

MISS M. How do you like that, Colonel
Honeywood ?

COL. H. Oh, I like it—yes, I like it ; yet
somehow, I don't know how it is, but there's
something about it I don't like.

MISS M. How inconsistent gentlemen are !
Like and don't like ! Well, I found it in a book
of old songs, and it took my fancy. "Ah ! sweetest
melancholy !" (*Aside.*) It seemed to be in keep-
ing with my thoughts.

COL. H. (*jauntily*) Oh, you are young, Cecilia,

nd have life before you ! Why should you be
ad ? Cheer up, cheer up ! I seem to have
ntered into a new existence since your dear
1amma persuaded you to listen to my suit.
Vhat happiness is before us ! (*She does not appear
> hear, and after a pause he adds.*) Why, what is
1e matter ? A penny for your thoughts, my dear !
Ia, ha, ha !

MISS M. I beg your pardon, Colonel, I'm sure.
t was most stupid of me, but I was going off in
sort of dream. *Happiness*, I think you said?
Vith you, I think you said? Oh, yes, yes, I see—
understand. I was quite forgetting myself.
Rises from the piano and joins MRS. M. *at window
> L. They talk sotto-voce.*)

COL. H. (*seating himself on sofa to* R. *and raising
is voice ; he speaks with an affected drawl*). By-
ye, seen anything of those people lately who
sed to be here so much ?

MISS M. Perhaps you mean our friends the
'ercivals ?

COL. H. Ah, to be sure, Percival was the
ame. Young man gone abroad, I hear.

MISS M. (*drawing nearer*) I believe so (*with
n assumed air of indifference*). Have you heard
here he is?

COL. H. (*rising*) Oh, no, no, no ! Some new
1atrimonial spec, suppose.

Miss M. (*rather warmly*) Indeed? I understood that he had gone on business.

Col. H. (*arching his brows significantly*) Just so.

Mrs. M. (*coming down*) Have you asked our dear Colonel, my darling Cecilia——

Miss M. Yes, mamma, but he doesn't appear to——

Col. H. Well, the truth is, I did not exactly like——

Mrs. M. Yes? (Miss M. *hangs upon his words.*)

Col. H. Did not like to repeat the story which goes about; but it is reported that Charles Percival is on the track of a great foreign heiress, with I don't know how much a year, and I don't know how much capital besides!

Mrs. M. Prodigious, my dear Colonel! (*imposes her hands.*)

Miss M. (*aside*) Oh! Charles! No hope, no hope!

Mrs. M. (*to* Miss M.) You ought to consider yourself very fortunate, my dearest, in having escaped from a man who evidently looks at marriage as a mere medium for improving his fortune. (*The* Colonel *seems a little uneasy;* Miss M. *smiles coldly and casts a side-glance at him.*) Give me the man who marries a girl for her own sake.

Miss M. (*aside*) This is almost too much.

Col. H. I am a great admirer of disinterestedness myself—(*aside*) especially in other people. If

I don't take care, this young fellow will bowl me out yet. I must give that girl of Cecilia's another refresher. A deuced dear game, egad! (*Retires up with a self-satisfied air, and leans out of window to* R.)

MRS. M. The sooner you are married, my darling Cecilia, the better, I think. Our dear Colonel is very anxious that there should be no further delay. I shall speak to your papa this evening, my dear.

MISS M. Where do you think, mamma, that the Colonel talks of taking me for the honeymoon? Oh, to the English Lakes. I have heard that they are not to be seen in full perfection till later on in the autumn. It would be a pity to hurry. (*Aside.*) If I could only gain a little time!

MRS. M. Your papa and I, my dear, are contemplating a tour this summer in Switzerland, and I should like to have your marriage over before we go away, darling. (*Aside.*) The little puss is temporising.

MISS M. (*half-reproachfully.*) So soon? I must entreat dearest papa to intercede for me. (*Aside.*) I will give Charles time, whatever it costs.

MRS. M. I know you too well, my dearest, to believe that you will oppose our wishes, your father's and mine.

MISS M. (*taking her mother's hand*) Has it not

been one of the studies of my life to obey you both, my dearest mother?

COL. H. (*returning from window*) I see papa coming; he looks as beaming as possible—in a downright good-humour.

MRS. M. (*aside*) I shall easily get him over to my way of thinking, then.

MISS M. (*aside*) I shall have no difficulty in coaxing him out of this hasty marriage, then.

Enter MR. MONTAGU *from* L. *They all advance to greet him. He kisses* MRS. *and* MISS MON- TAGU *and shakes hands with the* COLONEL.

MRS. M. My dear Cecil, you look hot.

MR. M. It's everybody's business to look hot in this sort of weather, my dear. Nobody has a right to look anything else. Colonel, what do you mean by looking so cool?

COL. H. Ha, ha! not so bad! not so bad! (*To* MRS. M.) He will have his joke!

MRS. M. My dear Cecil, I desire to speak with you for a moment. (MR. M. *appears the least trifle bored.*) Cecilia, my dear, leave us for a little; you can introduce our dear Colonel to some of the beauties of the prospect.

MISS M. (*aside*) A splendid prospect! Twenty square feet of what looks like brown paper in the distance, but turns out to be grass on a closer

inspection : a weeping ash, a parched poplar : and
two boxes of sundries !

> [MR. *and* MRS. MONTAGU *draw chairs to the
> front;* MISS MONTAGU *and* COLONEL
> HONEYWOOD *retire up, and converse at
> window seated.*

MR. M. Now, my dear, what is it ? No time to
lose.

MRS. M. My dear Cecil, you have the whole
evening before you.

MR. M. So I have—for dinner.

MRS. M. My dear Cecil, I have been telling our
dear girl that I am of opinion that the sooner she
is established the better it will be on all accounts.
Her mind is very unsettled at present.

MR. M. Hem ! Well, the man likes you, and
you like the man, and I like the man so-so. The
question is whether Cecilia likes the man, and
whether the man likes her ?

MRS. M. The Colonel is a man of excellent
position, and moves in the best society; what
more can you expect, my dear Cecil ? On suc-
ceeding to the property, he thinks that ministers
could not do less than restore him to the barony
of Glengarry. A coronet would set off our dear
girl's features admirably. She has just that sort
of face.

MR. M. (*dryly*) Not an uncommon sort of face, I believe. (*Turning round.*) What is that?

[*A tap is heard at the door to* L.; MISS MONTAGU *rises to open it; JEANNETTE puts a paper in her hand, which she glances at hastily, and then squeezes hurriedly into her pocket, her countenance brightening.*

MISS M. (*advancing*) Jeannette brought something for me, that was all. Did you see Charlie Percival before he went, papa?

MR. M. I did.

MISS M. Did he say where he was going to?

MR. M. He did.

MISS M. (*eagerly*) Where?

MR. M. He desired that it should not be known.

MISS M. But surely he would not mind our being told.

MR. M. It was his last request to me that, whomever I informed, I should not tell you!

MISS M. (*turning half away disappointed and distressed*) How strange! (*Aside.*) I would give my eyes to read that paper; it is a telegram—*from him.* How can I slip away? (*Retires midway up to* L. *with back to stage.*)

MRS. M. Perhaps you might take the Colonel into your little study, and talk about the settlements before dinner, my dear Cecil?

MR. M. (*facetiously*) After dinner is considered the best time for settlements, my dear.

MRS. M. This is a very important business, my dear Cecil; it is no joking matter.

MR. M. (*aside*). Decidedly serious for me. (*To* MISS M.) Well, what does Cecilia say?

MISS M. (*advancing to front*) I say that, for my own part, I cheerfully renounce all claim to the noble fortune which you inherited from grandpapa, and which you have increased so largely by your own industry. Leave it to charities; a more modest lot will satisfy me. Think of the great reward elsewhere, which would wait upon such a disposition of the estate hereafter. As far as the Colonel is concerned, supposing he were to honour me under the altered circumstances with his preference, I am sure you need fear no obstacle, for he has just told us that he is a great admirer of disinterestedness! (*The* COLONEL *glances sharply round for a moment unperceived.*)

MR. M. (*after a pause*) Do you hear this, Colonel?

COL. H. (*starting as if surprised*) Beg pardon! I was listening to the songs of the birds; I did not catch what was said. (*He leaves the window and comes down.*)

MR. M. Why, my daughter has been saying that she proposes to give up all her interest in my property, and desires me to bequeath it to charitable purposes; and she believes you will have no objection—that it will make no difference in your feelings?

Col. H. (*appearing to consider*). Well, that is my view—that is *quite* my view; yes, that is *entirely* my view. (*They all seem to be taken by surprise.*)

Mr. M. (*warmly*) Cecilia is a fine noble-hearted girl, and you are worthy of her. Cecilia, he loves you for your own sake, you see. (Miss M. *smiles and bows, but makes no reply.*)

Col. H. (*passionately*). For her own sake, dear girl! May I be permitted to have the honour? (*Stoops down, takes* Miss M.'s *hand, and raises it to his lips.*) (*Aside.*) Got out of those confounded settlements! A splendid fluke!

Mrs. M. My dear Cecil, after what has passed, I conclude the question may be regarded as settled?

Mr. M. I should almost prefer two or three days for final consideration, since this new point has been raised. (*Aside.*) Percival's month is up the day after to-morrow.

Miss M. (*aside*). Thank heaven! Charles may return before then.

Col. H. I will look in again—say, on Friday. Adieu, my dearest madam. Adieu, Cecilia. My

dear sir, *au revoir*. (*Shakes hands with them all.*)
(*Aside.*) Not a moment to be lost. [*Exit.*

[MISS M. *retires up and appears to look out of
window to* R. *She snatches the telegram
out of her pocket and reads it.*

MRS. M. (*folding her hands before her raptu-
rously.*) My dear Cecil, our dear Colonel's affection
for our dear girl is something beautiful. So unsel-
fish, so devoted! I quite look forward to Friday.
Let us hope that there will be no further delay.

MR. M. We shall see, my dear.

MISS M. (*aside, at window*). "All going well,"
he says; "keep up your spirits. Don't be pre-
cipitate." That's all; he doesn't say where he is
or when he will be back. How vexatious! (*Puts
the paper back in her pocket and turns to window.*)

MRS. M. Come, child, give me your arm; we
must be thinking of our toilettes. (MISS M. *comes
down.*) Why, you look quite grave. You ought
to be as happy as the day is long. You may be
Lady Glengarry yet; who knows? [*Exit to* L.

MISS M. Ah! who does? Wonders never
cease. (*Aside.*) The Colonel was too sharp for
me; I must try again. [*Exit after* MRS. M.

MR. M. (*solus*) My wife seems to be thoroughly
infatuated with the new notion. The Greek prince
and the rest of Ralph's friends have had their
congé, and the house rings with the praises of

Honeywood. He seems a simple-minded sort of man, without that eye to the main chance which one finds in people of the world. At any rate, Mrs. M. seems to have set her heart upon it, and if Cecilia does not revolt at the last moment, or that young Percival doesn't turn up, like the hero of a novel, just as the bride is going to be given away, and carry her off in triumph, I suppose it will be a match. Well, we shall see what we shall see, as we bankers have it. For my part, I don't much wonder at the girl hankering a bit after Charlie, as I half believe she does yet. If I was a young girl—but what's the use of speculating? [*Exit.*

CURTAIN.

SCENE 2.

The Bank of MONTAGU BROTHERS *at Rotterdam.* MR. RALPH MONTAGU'S *private apartment, looking over the principal quay. A breakfast-room with French windows and finished in the French style; view of the canal and shipping from windows.* CHARLES PERCIVAL *discovered alone, pacing the room.*

CHAS. P. I wonder what's going on at home! Honeywood won't leave a stone unturned to gain his object. He is a thorough man of the world; and not over-scrupulous, neither. I asked my uncle to look in at the Montagus' and telegraph me any news; but I know well enough he won't. He eyed me with an expression of the wildest consternation, when I told him, that a telegram wouldn't stand him in no more than a sovereign or so. That fellow has had time to announce me by this time! Ah! here he comes, I think.

Enter SERVANT.

SERV. My master's kind regards to you, sir, and will be down in five minutes; hopes you'll make yourself comfortable; quite expects you to remain to breakfast with him.

CHAS. P. Thankee, thankee. (*Exit* SERV.) Well, he does not forget me, at all events: the only son of his dearest friend Robert Percival. It's a bold stroke; but there's something which seems to tug at the skirts of my coat, whenever my heart fails me a little, and whispers in my ear, Venture and Win! Yet I feel deucedly nervous at times; I feel that if any one were only to cry, *Ha!* it would frighten me out of my wits. (MR. RALPH MON-TAGU *enters unperceived, and slaps* CHAS. P. *on the shoulder.*)

MR. RALPH MONT. Ha!

CHAS. P. Ho! Good gracious, how you frightened

E

me! I didn't hear you coming. The sea-voyage
has——

MR. R. M. Ah! I shouldn't wonder; it often
does. Well, what wind blew you here? How did you
leave them all—your excellent uncle, my brother,
and the rest of them? I am really delighted to
see you. No, I don't find you altered in the least,
except that you are taller and bigger, and have
taken to wearing trousers, which makes a difference. You haven't breakfasted?

CHAS. P. Well, no——

R. M. That's right; we'll have a chat over tea
and toast. I live, you know, in the good old
English fashion. Well, I'm very pleased to see
you.

SERVANT *enters and lays breakfast.*

CHAS. P. (*in a hesitating manner*) Thanks,
thanks. I—I was in this neighbourhood — I
mean, I was in Holland, and I—I thought I
would look in.

MR. M. I should have been very much concerned indeed, if my dear friend's son had come
my way, without doing so.

CHAS. P. Yes, of course—I should never have
thought of coming round this way without looking
in. (*Aside.*) What a devil of a mess I'm getting
into. (*Aloud.*) I shall really enjoy my breakfast.
The sea-air——

Mr. M. I always found it so myself. What'll ye take? I can recommend that. The coffee'll be here directly. Pray, begin.

Chas. P. Thanks. Oh! I left Mr. Cecil and his family much the same as usual, and as to my uncle, I don't think you'd see any great alteration.

Mr. M. A good man, your uncle, a very good man; but, if my memory does not fail me, I have sometimes known him odd.

Chas. P. (*aside*). So have I.

Mr. M. But, Lord bless me, we all have our faults.

Chas. P. True, true. Ah! you were inquiring what wind blew me here? (Mr. M. *assents.*) Well, I must tell you: a little business affair.

Mr. M. If I can be of use to you, command me. (*They rise. and bring chairs to front.*)

Chas. P. Thanks. To tell you the truth, my dear sir, I'm thinking of going into business.

Mr. M. You *do* surprise me. (*Aside.*) He has evidently heard I'm thinking of a partner.

Chas. P. Commercial life will be an agreeable change. I'm tired of knocking about.

Mr. M. But your uncle is very well off?

Chas. P. (*hesitatingly*) Oh! y-es, yes.

Mr. M. And will leave you everything?

Chas. P. Y-es, yes; I've no reason to suppose otherwise.

Mr. M. And in the meantime makes you a handsome allowance, no doubt?

Chas. P. (*dubiously*) Yes—yes—oh, yes, he *does*.

Mr. M. What more, then, d'ye want?

Chas. P. You see I'm getting on, Mr. Montagu, one can't be always young; and I want to settle, in short; in short, I wish, in short, to get married, in short.

Mr. M. A lady in the case! Of course, your uncle would be prepared to lay down a fair sum for the purchase of a share in some first-class house?

Chas. P. Well, I don't know. (*Aside.*) He has heard that I am on the look-out for a partnership.

Mr. M. You've some friend, then, who would advance the money?

Chas. P. I don't know anybody.

Mr. M. Your father-in-law proposes to help you, I presume?

Chas. P. He gives me his daughter.

Mr. M. (*smiling*) A very precious gift, I've no doubt, Charles, but hardly a negociable security!

Chas. P. I· submit, sir, that that may depend on circumstances. (*Aside.*) He's evidently pumping me!

Mr. M. I understand you; she is an only child.

(CHAS. P. *bows assent.*) (*Aside.*) Hem! Something in that! (*To* CHAS. P.) Rich people, I presume?

CHAS. P. One of the wealthiest families in London. (*Aside.*) I must not let him see all my hand at once.

MR. M. Hem! (*Aside.*) It won't do to seem too eager. (*To* CHAS. P.) When, pray, does the affair come off—your union with this lady?'

CHAS. P. When I have obtained my partnership.

MR. M. If I put you in the way of getting what you desire, what guarantee would you be prepared with? An ante-nuptial settlement to a suitable amount would meet the case. I must be armed with full particulars, my boy, full particulars, or I can't act.

CHAS. P. You have a partner for me in your eye, then, Mr. Montagu?

MR. M. (*musing*) Well, I have. I think I know a gentleman, who would not object to the introduction of new blood and additional capital into his business—of course, if proper security was forthcoming.

CHAS. P. Quite so. My father-in-law *in futuro* is a banker of old standing.

MR. M. Strangely enough, my friend is precisely in the same line of business.

CHAS. P. The house is commonly reported to

be worth half-a-dozen millions, and to have an income of £400,000 a year.

Mr. M. (*aside*) We should just double our capital. (*To* Chas. P.) Commonly reported, a-hem! Six millions, a-hem! £400,000 a year, a-hem! Would it be premature to mention names?— (*Observes that he is embarrassed.*) Ah yes, probably, probably.

Chas. P. The gentleman, whom you propose to introduce to me, my kind friend, might, if it did not trespass too much on his time, accompany me back to London, and judge for himself. The whole thing, I undertake, could be settled in half-an-hour.

Mr. M. I'm going to London, by a remarkable coincidence, in a few days; suppose we all travel together? (*Aside.*) I shall surprise him, when I shew him his partner!

Chas. P. Agreed—oh! of course, with the greatest pleasure, my dear sir. (*Aside.*) He'll be rather astonished, when I present him to the lady! (*To* Mr. M.) You've a nice view from the window, by-the-bye. (*Retires up, and looks out.*)

Mr. M. Ah, yes. (*Aside.*) Who would ever have dreamt of this young fellow, whom I haven't seen or heard of for twelve years or more, turning up so unexpectedly, and, above all, coming to consult me on the very subject, which I had uppermost in my mind? The figures are heavy, decidedly so; but what of that? as we bankers have it, so much the better. Not that we want money. Not that we don't! I shall have to institute strict inquiries, when I get to town, but of course my brother will be well acquainted with the parties. I don't know how it is, that these young chaps get hold of the young girls! I never get hold of them! However, it's not a bad morning's work altogether. (*Slaps his knee approvingly.*)

CHAS. P. (*coming briskly down*) My dear sir, nothing serious, I hope?

MR. M. Serious? Oh! dear no. I merely slapped my knee; it's a thing I do sometimes.

[CHAS. P. *seats himself in front;* MR. M. *rises, and retires slowly up to window.*

CHAS. P. (*aside*) Who would have thought that I should have pulled through so easily? Not I, for one! It is the most extraordinary piece of luck that I ever met with. I'm hanged if it's not rather suspicious! He evidently wants to get a partner. Why does he want to get a partner, that's the question? But no! absurd! it can't be. The only thing is, I'm a deuced fortunate fellow. By Jove, I feel almost beside myself with joy. (*Laughs out.*) [MR. MONTAGU *returns down.*

MR. M. What's the matter?

CHAS. P. Matter? I was only laughing at something that struck me. It's a thing I do sometimes!

MR. M. (*smiling somewhat disconcertedly*) Oh!
—Well, when shall we start?

CHAS. P. I'm completely at the service of your friend and yourself.

MR. M. Suppose we say the day after to-morrow?

CHAS. P. Good.

MR. M. Meanwhile, you must make my house your home. I shall shew you all the lions of Rotterdam.

CHAS. P. Thanks, thanks.

MR. M. Come and see my conservatory and books, will you?

CHAS. P. With the greatest pleasure. (*Aside.*) The only literature I care about just now is a deed of partnership, original MS. on vellum, as they say in the catalogues, very legibly written. [*Exeunt.*

CURTAIN.

ACT IV.

· Scene i.

Morning-room at the Percivals'. Mr. Percival, Senior, *discovered in his dressing-gown at breakfast, turning over the leaves of a Bradshaw.*

Mr. P. Well, there's Mayence! One hears a good deal about Mayence. Egad! I'll go to Mayence for my autumn tour. No! I won't. There's the South of France. What's-his-name told me he lived capitally for eighteen-pence a day, including *vin du pays*, at what's-its-name. Egad! that's not a bad idea. No! They talk a good deal about Buxton; never been there; egad! I'll try it. No! I dare say it'll be confoundedly expensive; I won't go anywhere. I hate the sea: it makes one sick. I hate railways; they're organised swindles. I hate coaches; they're a detestable affectation of— thingamy. I hate walking; it sets one's corns in a flame. I hate riding; the saddle wears out one's things——

Enter SERVANT.

Eh?

SERV. A gentleman, sir, wishes to see you.

MR. P. Has he no name?

SERV. I don't think he has, sir. At least, I mean——

MR. P. What the devil *do* you mean, you blockhead?

SERV. I mean he only called himself *a gentleman*, but he's the same party that called himself Colonel Honeywood, when he came here before.

MR. P. Why the devil didn't you tell me that at first?

SERV. Because I thought he was making an *incognito* of himself——

MR. P. Does he ask to see me?

SERV. He asks to see my master; I says to him, Which my master, the Senior or the Junior? He wishes my eyes bad luck, and says, MISTER Percival; I don't know, he says, anything about any other master——

MR. P. Ah! Shew him up, shew him up. Why the devil don't you shew him up?

SERV. Going, sir. (*Steps back.*) Did you understand me, sir, that the gentleman used violent language?

MR. P. Yes, what of that?

SERV. He swore at me, sir.

MR. P. (*raising his voice*) Did he, sir ?

SERV. (*energetically*) He damned my eyes, sir.

MR. P. (*still louder*) I'm very glad to hear it, sir. Be off with you, and tell him to walk in, or I'll do the same.

SERV. (*aside*) Give me these aristocracy to swear ! (*Holds up his hands, and exit.*)

MR. P. Now I shall get some news of Charles, no doubt. The young rascal hasn't written to me, since he left. A good-hearted lad, but horribly eccentric.

Enter COLONEL HONEYWOOD *from* L., *hat in hand, bowing deferentially. Hastens up to* MR. P.

COL. H. My dear sir, don't rise. (*They shake fingers.*) It rejoices me to see you well. But you are breakfasting—it may be inconvenient ?

MR. P. Thankee, no, I've done. (*Aside.*) Dare say he came with the idea——

COL. H. I presume you've heard from your dear nephew, my dear sir? (*Aside.*) Shouldn't wonder if he thought——

MR. P. No, sir, I have not.

COL. H. He must be enjoying himself immensely. (*Rubs his hands.*)

MR. P. Not in a position to say.

COL. H. A pure matter of recreation, of course.

MR. P. Well, I believe he had some object as

well. (*Aside.*) I hope he'll succeed in it, too, and be able to repay me my ten pounds.

COL. H. Ah! combining business with pleasure! What does the poet say? *Utile Dulci!* (*Aside.*) The old fool doesn't know anything about it evidently!

MR. P. Ah! (*Aside.*) The old fool thinks I'm going to tell him all I know!

COL. H. Mine has been a varied career, Mr. Percival, do you know?

MR. P. (*languidly*) Indeed!

COL. H. I may call it romantic almost. (MR. P. *seems a little bored.*) Do you know how I began life?

MR. P. Not unless you began it by being born!

COL. H. Ah, very good, very good indeed. You remind me of your dear nephew——

MR. P. Do I?

COL. H. Very much, my dear sir; he's a dry dog.

MR. P. Then I suppose I'm to conclude that I'm a dry dog, too?

COL. H. (*apologetically*) I would not for a moment permit myself to suggest such a thing. I merely spoke figuratively.

MR. P. I see.

COL. H. Well, I began life by robbing an orchard——

MR. P. A bad commencement, but a good ending.

COL. H. (*pleasantly inquisitive*) How's that, how's that?

MR. P. I mean that people who start by robbing orchards often come to higher preferment (*performs a dumb-show descriptive of a man being hanged*).

COL. H. (*warmly*) Mr. Percival, is that an insinuation?

MR. P. (*coolly*) No, I merely spoke *figuratively*.

COL. H. (*looking rather foolish*) I see. Well, my dear sir (*recovers his usual manner*), what should you say now, if I told you that I was going to be married?

MR. P. 'Pon my word, I don't know.

COL. H. But what *would* you say?

MR. P. I think I should say, Oh!

COL. H. Hem!—to a very pretty girl?

MR. P. At your time of life—I should say, No.

COL. H. Hem!—of very large expectations?

MR. P. That alters the case.

COL. H. And whom you know very well indeed —Miss Montagu!

MR. P. Miss Montagu? By Jingo!—(*Restrains himself on consideration.*)

Enter SERVANT *bearing a letter.*

SERV. Telegram, sir. [*Exit.*

MR. P. (*opening it*) Ah! from Charles. Excuse
me. (*Reads to himself, the* COLONEL *manœuvring
all the time to endeavour to catch a glimpse of the
contents.*) "C. Percival at Rotterdam to H. Percival,
Esq., at London. Detained unexpectedly two
days. Gain time for me at any price." (*Aside.*)
Dear, dear, dear! The devil! the devil! Ah! I
have a good idea.

COL. H. Intelligence about our young friend
abroad perfectly satisfactory, I hope? (*Endeavours
to edge himself round so as to get a sight of the paper,
which* MR. P. *holds loosely in his hand.*)

MR. P. (*after a slight pause*) To tell the truth,
not quite so satisfactory as I could wish. He
writes to me from—let me see—ah, Zurich, to
say that he is ill, and wants me to go over to him.
But my own engagements make such a thing
impossible—impossible. Now, it has just occurred
to me, that you might feel disposed—to take a trip
—next to myself, perhaps, there is no one for
whom my nephew entertains a warmer regard—
and as for your expenses—of course, you must
consider me your banker—what d'ye say? (*Puts
telegram in his pocket.*)

COL. H. This news is very distressing, my dear
sir. (*Aside.*) Rather opportune! out of the way
just at the right moment! (*Aloud.*) My only
doubt is as to time. This affair of mine comes

off in a week. I should not be able to spare more than a couple of days——

Mr. P. That would do capitally—I was just going to mention a couple of days. (*Aside.*) He would be out of the way just at the right time! (*Aloud.*) When will you go?

Col. H. This evening, of course.

Mr. P. Come and dine with me, and then you can start afterwards; I shall make a point of seeing you off. You may be considerably out of pocket; so I will give you fifty pounds for your expenses, when we meet on the boat; and will order my bankers to see that you have fifty more, when you get to your destination.

Col. H. (*indifferently*) Oh, that's of no consequence; any time will do. (*Aside.*) About twenty 'll answer my needs; twenty 'll stop Chorley's mouth, till the thing's over; and the rest's all swag. (*Aloud.*) I shall see you again; for the present, adieu! [*Exit to* L.

Mr. P. (*solus*) Ah! I'll put it down, while I think of it. (*Takes out a pocket-book, and writes:*) Memo.—£100 to Col. H. for C. P.—Zurich.— To ask C. P. to repay same—say, by one hundred yearly instalments.—To tell James not to let the Colonel in, when he returns from what's-it's-name —to see Monta——

Enter SERVANT *from* R.

MR. P. ——gu. Eh? (*Pushes the book into his pocket.*)

SERV. Mr. Montagu, sir, wishes to see you.

MR. P. (*aside*) Curious coincidence, egad! One goes out, and t'other walks in. It looks as if one was rather in request, egad! (*To* SERV.) Shew Mr. What's-his-name in.

SERV. Yes, sir.   [*Exit.*

MR. P. (*solus*) There may be some confederacy, egad! I must be on my guard. (*Buttons up his trousers' pockets.*)

Enter MR. MONTAGU *from* R.

MR. M. (*advancing briskly*) I'm truly pleased to see you again, sir. I hope you're well?

MR. P. Ah! thankee, so-so. (*They shake hands.*) (*Aside.*) I don't altogether like this cordiality.

MR. M. We seem quite strangers; I hope it won't be so for the future!

MR. P. Ah! well, I don't know how it is. I— yes, well—(*Aside.*) He's leading up to something.

MR. M. (*taking a chair*) Affairs in the City, for the last three months, have been extremely critical, my dear sir.

MR. P. (*taking a chair, and aside*) He has heard that I have put by a few pounds, and has come to borrow them! (*Feels his pockets.*)

Mr. M. But I am very thankful to say, that our house has passed through the difficulty quite un-scathed.

Mr. P. I'm delighted to hear it. (*Grasps him by the hand.*) (*Aside.*) Vast relief!

Mr. M. You see, sir, our firm is one of those old-established businesses——

Mr. P. Which are literally independent of commercial fluctuations, you were going to say. I understand you, I understand you.' (*Aside.*) I feel much more comfortable.

Mr. M. It really takes a great deal to touch an establishment which——

Mr. P. Has more than six millions of capital. I understand you, my dear sir, I understand you (*Aside.*) One must approach one's subject delicately.

Mr. M. (*smiling*) Well, you seem to have our balance-sheet at your fingers' ends; however, the capital of the larger City houses is pretty well known as a rule, I believe, within a few thousands. I shall not dispute your figures. But the fact is that what I particularly wished to refer to, the point indeed, to say the honest truth, on which I came here to consult you (Mr. P. *resumes for a moment his former expression of solicitude*), was the sort of understanding your nephew, my old-young friend Charles, arrived at with me, when we were last together. I was to hear from him in a month

F

from that time, whether or no he could negotiate a certain advantageous partnership in some house abroad; an important question for us both hinges on this; and Master Charles's time is up to-morrow. Is he on his return, pray?

MR. P. He telegraphed to me to-day—I had the message an instant ago—just as you came in. Two days, he said, would see him here.

MR. M. The day after to-morrow. How vexing! I have promised to give another gentleman a decisive answer on Wednesday morning—a gentleman, who is also a suitor for my daughter's hand. You know him—Colonel Honeywood?

MR. P. Ah, yes. But is a day so important?

MR. M. Pardon me, sir, a London banker's word is his bond.

MR. P. I think I see a way of removing your scruples completely.

MR. M. (*a little eagerly*) How?

MR. P. Honeywood will not call on you to-morrow to fulfil his engagement.

MR. M. You surprise me. Explain.

MR. P. Nothing more easy; he has left the country.

MR. M. Left the country? I'm amazed.

MR. P. He starts for Zurich this very day in search of my nephew. (*Aside.*) He'll be a long time finding him there. (*Aloud.*) He goes on my own account; I handed him not long since his expenses. (*Aside.*) Moving a little !

Mr. M. Dear, dear ! you take my breath away almost. I can scarcely believe my ears. However, all that I can say is, that, as both the gentlemen are likely by your account to be behindhand, the first-comer shall have the lady, so far as I am concerned.

Mr. P. Is that a bargain, sir ?

Mr. M. A bargain—so far as I am concerned. Mrs. Montagu and the Colonel are great friends, let me tell you; but I won't answer for it that Charles, if he comes home with a partnership in his pocket, will not carry the day even in that quarter. I conclude your nephew has spoken to you freely about this ? What facilities has he, let me ask, for obtaining what he seeks ? In my young days, such prizes were few and far between.

Mr. P. To be frank with you, I haven't a ghost of a notion. He asked me for ten pounds, and said, " Leave the rest to me."

Mr. M. Well, we shall see what we shall see, sir. Ah ! Mr. Percival, Mr. Percival, you know all about it——

Mr. P. I assure you——

Mr. M. Ah ! well, I don't blame you ; you're perfectly right. Let me see, what was I going to say ? Oh ! I was going to say that Honeywood is a gentleman by birth and education, and heir, as he tells us, to a peerage. (MR. P. *smiles sceptically.*) Ah! well, that may be so, or may not. (*Rises to go.*) Good day to you.   [*Exit.*

MR. P. What a deuced bore, having to make oneself agreeable for the sake of one's posterity!

[*Exit.*

CURTAIN.

SCENE 2.

Park-avenue of MR. MONTAGU'S *country residence at Streatham. A vista of trees up. Gates of house seen midway up to* L.

Enter MISS MONTAGU, *apparently in a very distressed state of mind, through gates to* L.

MISS M. Oh dear, what shall I, shall I do? The dreadful day is close at hand. It seems to hang over me like a drawn sword. I cannot bear the sight of this Colonel Honeywood, and half that he tells us about himself I believe in my heart is a wicked story. Yet my mother is infatuated with him: he holds her in a complete spell. Oh! Charles, Charles, why do you not come, and save me? Ah! how strange everything looks! (*Faints.*)

Enter MRS. MONTAGU, *from* R.

MRS. M. (*rushing forward with her hands expanded as usual*) What is it, what is it? (*Receives* MISS M. *in her arms.*) Help! help!

MISS M. (*rallying*) I'm better now, I shall be all right presently. I feel quite strong again, I do, indeed I do. There, don't go for any one. I was only a little faint for the moment; it is a sensation which comes over me now and then. The fresh air will take it away.

MRS. M. Lean on my arm, my child, and let us return into the house.

MISS M. I think, mother, the pleasant breeze, which has just sprung up, will do me more good, I do.

MRS. M. It is nothing more than excitement at the delightful look-out before you, my darling Cecilia. The happy day draws near. I have no doubt that our dear Colonel will be here to-day to sign the necessary papers; he ought to have been with us yesterday; but you cannot expect rigid punctuality from men of such high position. Ah! my dearest Cecilia, our dear Colonel is one of those rare beings——

MISS M. (*interrupting peevishly.*) Oh! let us talk of something else, dearest mother. When do you fancy that Charles will be back?

MRS. M. (*drawing herself up*) Charles Percival?

I don't know, I am sure. I believe Charles Percival, my dear, to be an adventurer and a visionary.
Our dear Colonel is a man of very different stamp ;
a gentleman in every sense of the word, my dear,
and I should not at all wonder, if he made you
Lady Glengarry some day——

Miss M. But Charles, mother, is going to get
a partnership, and then——

Mrs. M. And then ? A partnership, indeed !
A fiddledee ! It is my belief, my dear, that this mis-
guided young man (Miss M. *bites her lip*) has gone
abroad solely that he may come back with some
cock-and-a-bull-story, and persuade your father to
agree to his proposal. But he won't persuade *Me*,
my dear. Never ! (*Draws herself majestically up.*)

Miss M. (*aside*) Is it not enough to make one
undutiful ? Hark ! I hear some one approaching !

Enter Mr. Montagu.

Mr. M. Well, ladies, what do you think is the
latest news ?   (Mrs. *and* Miss M. *look inquiringly.*)
Charles Percival returned from abroad yesterday.

Mrs. M. In charge, I hope, of our dear
Colonel ?

Mr. M. You are mistaken, my dear; he is
accompanied by the gentleman who has accepted
him as a partner.

Mrs. M. Who may this gentleman be, pray ?

Mr. M. He does not name him, but says that, when we meet, he will explain everything.

Mrs. M. Some Continental impostor, I have no doubt, who is in league with these Percivals to entrap our dear Cecilia into a fatal marriage.

Miss M. (*aside*) Oh ! for shame !

Mr. M. A very pleasant supposition, my dear, but I'm sorry to say that, so far as we are at present advised, it is entirely gratuitous. I have just received a letter from Charles to say, that he is on his way here to pay his respects to us, and to introduce the gentleman who accompanies him.

Mrs. M. Some foreigner of distinction, my dear Cecil, I make no question. Well, well, bear in mind that our poor girl's future happiness hangs upon this ! The Continent swarms with pretended grandees, my dear——

Miss M. (*archly*) Such as Prince Rhodomontados and Baron Butterbrode, do you mean, mother? (Mrs. M. *bows benignly, not having heard.*)

Mr. M. (*playfully*) You saucy puss ! Your Uncle Ralph should hear you !

Enter Mr. Percival, Sen., *from* r. *He appears to be unusually cheerful, wears his hat on the back of his head, and brandishes an umbrella about.* Mr. P. *shakes hands with them all successively.*

Mr. P. (*removing his hat, which he keeps in his*

hand). And how d'ye do? And how do *you* do? And how do you *do ?*

MR. M. (*jocularly for him*) Why, Percival, you're cutting capers like a blue lamb at an election meeting! I would to heaven, man, I'd got half your spirits.

MR. P. Ah! well—ye see—yes—ah !—(*Aside.*) I see my way to getting my hundred pound back much clearer than I did yesterday, by gum !

MISS M. We are expecting Charles and the gentleman whom he has brought with him, Mr. Percival, almost directly. Have you seen Mr.— Mr.——?

MR. P. No, my dear young friend, I've *not* seen Mr.—Mr.——

MRS. M. (*aside*) Of course, a mere man of straw, as I suspected.

MR. P. I beg your pardon, madam?

MRS. M. (*blandly*) I am afraid that you will catch cold without your hat.

MR. M. Suppose we go in, then. Percival, we can give you a bed to-night.

MR. P. Thankee, thankee.

MR. M. Charles and his friend 'll be here by dinner-time at latest. We shall be quite a pleasant party.

MRS. M. I wonder where our dear Colonel is.

MR. P. (*chuckling*) Oh ! ma'am, he's enjoying

himself in the best inn at Zurich by this time. (*Aside.*) Confound him! at my expense, too.

MRS. M. He's too much of a gentleman, I'm sure, not to keep his engagement. I shall wait dinner for him. [*Exit into house.*

MR. M. (*aside*) I shan't. (*Follows her.*)

MISS M. Oh! Mr. Percival, when do you think that the two gentlemen will be here? We shall be *so* pleased to see Charles again. It seems quite an age since he left. He will come back so proud with his partnership, that he will scarcely deign to speak to poor little me!

MR. P. My dear, be assured that he will be the same as ever. Don't tell me, don't tell me (*shaking his finger at her playfully*); I know what I know. Ha, ha! (*Exeunt into house also.*)

A man, suddenly restored to consciousness, enters at back from R. *stealthily, walking on tiptoe. He looks round him, and then beckons to somebody behind. Enter a second man in a greatcoat, with a handkerchief wrapped round his throat for partial concealment. He approaches the first circumspectly. They both presently retreat on hearing a sound of advancing footsteps without speaking. It appears to get darker.*

Enter CHARLES PERCIVAL *from* L.

CHAS. P. (*looking about him*) Well, there's no

one here, after all. I certainly thought, as I walked up the drive, that I saw some one or other, and I took it to be him. He ought to be here to meet me. He must have lost his way, confound it ! I will go and look. [*Exit.*

CURTAIN.

SCENE 3.

Boudoir at MR. MONTAGU'S, *Russell Square ; a family group,* MR., MRS., *and* MISS MONTAGU *discovered, the former seated and conversing, the last pacing the room slowly. Immediately the curtain has risen,* COLONEL HONEYWOOD *introduces himself, and hurries up to* MRS. MONTAGU. *She greets him cordially,* MR. *and* MISS MONTAGU *are more distant.*

COL. H. My dearest madam, I trust I have not inconvenienced you by this slight delay? You're looking charming—as usual, my dear lady, as usual. How do you do, my dear Ce——Miss Montagu—if I may judge from appearances, never bonnier. And you, my dear sir?

MR. M. (*formally*) Pretty well, I thank you very much. I must implore you——

COL. H. Do not condemn me unheard, my dear sir. I was going to explain.

MR. M. I must implore you——

MRS. M. Let the Colonel at least speak, my dear Cecil. I am surprised at you, my dear.

COL. H. The fact is, my kind friends, that we had a terrible passage in the steamer, and had to put back, and lie by for several hours, or I should have been here yesterday. (*Aside.*) Can anything have got abroad?

MR. M. (*rather coldly*) Indeed! Just so! (*Aside.*) A pretty dilemma I'm in!

MISS M. How very disagreeable, to be sure! (*Aside.*) Another complication, I declare, when everything seemed to be going on smoothly! There's no getting rid of this dreadful man.

COL. H. (*with affected diffidence*) I seem to feel as if I was in a somewhat awkward situation, a-hem! I fear I'm intruding? (MR. *and* MISS M. *do not dissent.*)

MRS. M. Surely you jest, my dear Colonel? Most delighted to see you once more among us, are we not, my dear Cecil? (MR. M. *acquiesces ambiguously.*) Be seated, pray?

COL. H. Thank you very much; you look younger than ever, my dear madam. (*Seats himself.*) The fact is, we had a very bad passage in the boat——

Mr. M. (*dryly*) I think I recollect your making the observation before?

Col. H. Ah! to be sure; how ridiculous of me, now! But I was going to say, that I went to Zurich——

Mrs. M. In Holland?

Mr. M. My dear, don't expose your ignorance unnecessarily. Don't you know that Zurich is in Italy?

Col. H. So I thought, till I found it was in Switzerland. (Mr. *and* Mrs. M. *exchange looks.*) Well, I went there on a sleeveless errand for our friend Percival, who said that his nephew, young Charlie Percival, was laid up there at the sign of the *Golden Fleece.* When I got there, devil a bit Golden Fleece I found, and of course devil a bit Charles Percival. The whole thing was a hoax.

Mrs. M. I call that a very ungentlemanly deception, my dear Colonel. Confiding people like you and me are terribly imposed on by designing persons, who shall be nameless.

Mr. M. At any rate, Honeywood, you'll be sorry to hear, that poor Charlie has been in real danger from severe injuries he lately received.

Col. H. No?' Where? How?

Mr. M. Why, outside our own house at Streatham, the other night—the other evening, rather, for it was scarcely dark—he was assailed by two cowardly ruffians, and nearly strangled. They were startled by a noise, and made off, leaving the poor boy half dead on the ground.

COL. H. (*losing colour and voice*) No!

MR. M. One of them, a fellow of the name of Chorley, an innkeeper in the Borough, has been apprehended at Rochester; but his companion has not yet been found. It is hoped that Chorley will turn Queen's evidence.

MISS M. (*aside*). Poor Charles!

MRS. M. Rash young man!

COL. H. I am truly concerned, my kind friends. I think I saw some account of the matter in the papers; but, if I recollect, no names were mentioned?

MRS. M. Perhaps not; I dare say you will like to be left alone, you gentlemen. Come, Cecilia, my child, we will take a turn in our little garden.

> [*The ladies rise and exeunt, bowing to* COLONEL HONEYWOOD, *who rises, and opens the door for them.*

COL. H. (*aside, returning to his seat*) Atrocious predicament! I must lie close—I trust, my dear sir (*to* MR. M.), that the slight delay——

MR. M. Oh, do not mention it, Colonel; but, to be frank with you, the fact is, that—that—I—I—

*The door is quietly opened, and a man dressed in
plain black enters. He walks up straight to
COLONEL HONEYWOOD, who rises mechanically.*

STRANGER. I am a superintendent of police, and
hold a warrant for your apprehension, Captain
Slingsby. Resistance is useless; I have help close
at hand. You're wanted on a charge of treason-
felony and assault.

COL. H. (*with self-possession*) What do you
mean, sir, by this proceeding?

MR. M. There must be some mistake, sir; this
gentleman's name is not Slingsby. This is Colonel
Honeywood?

OFFICER (*smiling*). Doesn't make any difference,
sir, what he calls himself—Honeywood, or Slingsby,
or Crocker, or Fullarton, or half-a-dozen others.
(*To* COL. H.) Are you ready, Captain? I'm a
little pressed.

Enter MRS. and MISS M. in great excitement.

MRS. M. What's the meaning of all this? I
demand an explanation. Cecil! Colonel! You
sir! (MR. M. *and* COL. H. *are too much preoccupied
to answer.*)

OFFICER (*to* MRS. M.) I am a police officer,
ma'am, and have arrested this gentleman, Captain
Slingsby, by virtue of a warrant. Here it is.
(*Holds it before her.*)

COL. H. I shall *not* go; look to yourself. (*Pulls out a revolver and fires three times at the officer, but misses him.*)

OFFICER. Here, Robinson! Cleasby! Come in.

Two Constables rush in and seize COLONEL HONEY-WOOD *after a severe struggle.* MRS. MONTAGU *faints, and is carried out between* MISS MON-TAGU *and* MR. MONTAGU. *Exeunt Police with* COLONEL HONEYWOOD *handcuffed.*

Re-enter MR. MONTAGU *and* MISS MONTAGU.

MR. M. Does your mother seem better, my dear?

MISS M. Oh, yes, papa; she has been terribly shaken, though, by this extraordinary business. Did you ever know such a thing?

MR. M. All my other feelings are drowned in my thankfulness for your escape, my girl. In the world, we never know, you see, whom we harbour, who are our friends, or what our friends are, scarcely. However——

Enter SERVANT.

SERV. Mr. Ralph Montagu, sir, and Mr. Charles Percival.

MR. M. (*aside*) My brother! I did not know he was coming to England! (*To* SERV.) Oh, shew them up, of course.

Enter RALPH MONTAGU *and* CHARLES PERCIVAL. *The brothers greet each other cordially.* RALPH MONTAGU *kisses* CECILIA. *The latter gives both her hands to* CHARLES PERCIVAL. *The two brothers converse together for a moment in an undertone, explaining by gestures what has just occurred, &c., and also* CHARLES PERCIVAL *and* MISS MONTAGU.

Re-enter MRS. MONTAGU, *fanning herself briskly, and not appearing to notice any one.*

MRS. M. A pretty exposure! A pretty disgrace! I'm quite sure that I shall never get over it. Never.

RALPH M. (*advancing*) Well, you don't seem to see me, my dear.

MRS. M. (*with affected wonder*) Can I trust my eyes? Is that you, Ralph? (*They shake hands.*) When did you come over?

R. M. Yesterday only; partly on my own business, and partly on this young gentleman's. (*Points to* CHAS. P.)

MRS. M. What, you returned? I had no idea of it. (*They shake hands.*) You see us in a moment of sad confusion——

CHAS. P. Ah! poor Colonel——

MRS. M. Don't mention his name; he has terribly deceived us. What is more, I'm afraid

he'll be hanged. (*They all turn round to her*) Yes,
I'm afraid so, and next to being hanged oneself,
the worst thing in the world is to have an acquaint
ance hanged. People talk so !

CHAS. P. (*to* MR. M.) The circumstances, sir,
are somewhat distressing, but I think I must avail
myself of the present opportunity to communicate
to you and all those who are here, the successful
result of my journey. I have accomplished, Mr.
Montagu, the purpose with which I set out. I
now call upon you to perform your part of the
engagement. Allow me to introduce you to my
partner, Mr. Ralph Montagu, of Rotterdam !

MR. M. My brother ?

MISS M. (*wonderingly*) Uncle Ralph ?

CHAS. P. And, Mr. Ralph Montagu, now let
me introduce you to the lady. Miss Montagu—
Mr. Ralph Montagu !

R. M. My niece ?

MRS. M. Cecilia ?

MR. M. (*to* MRS. M. *and* R. M.) This youngster
has been too sharp for us, you see ; he has outwitted
us all ; and I am not sure it isn't for the best.

CHAS. P. (*to* R. M.) I told you, that if I could
procure a partnership, I had an opportunity of
marrying a lady of good expectations ? (*All look
towards* MISS M., *who hangs her head down in
confusion.*)

R. M. Yes; I had better confess at once that I swallowed the bait.

CHAS. P. (*to* MR. M.) And you may recollect, perhaps, my dear sir, that you promised, if I was successful in obtaining a share in a good concern abroad, you would waive your only objection to our union, and stand my friend?

MR. M. I did, I did.

MRS. M. May I ask, why *I* was not consulted throughout this delicate negotiation?

CHAS. P. I will deal with you in perfect frankness, my dear Mrs. Montagu. I knew that you had been prejudiced against me—that you were strongly prepossessed in favour of Colonel Honeywood, *as he called himself,* and that it was of no use for me to put forward my suit to you——

MR. M. Well, certainly, there was a time when my wife thought that Colonel Honeywood, *as he calls himself*——

MRS. M. There, there, my dear Cecil; I have been punished quite severely enough, I'm sure. Spare my feelings. I judged wrongly, I allow, my dear Cecil.

CHAS. P. That man, who would have ruined me, if he could, has met his deserts.

MR. M. And you have met yours, Charles. (*He takes his daughter's hand.*) She loves you, my boy, and you are worthy of her. You have our free consent to your marriage. (*Puts her hand in* CHARLES PERCIVAL'S.)

CHAS. P. Gratitude and joy choke my utterance. (*Silently takes* MISS MONTAGU'S *hand, and raises it to his lips.*)

Enter SERVANT.

SERV. (*to* MRS. M.) A jeweller is downstairs, ma'am. He has come with Mr. Percival senior's compliments, to bring a tray of rings for Miss Montagu's inspection. (*Exit -amid a general murmur of surprise.*)

Enter another SERVANT.

2nd SERV. (*to* MISS M.) A large parcel of perfumery has arrived from Rimmel's, Miss, for you, with Mr. Percival senior's compliments. (*Renewed expressions of astonishment and pleasure.*) There is also a person with a box of India shawls for your selection; he has orders to leave them till it suits yours convenience, Miss, to look at them.

[*Exit.*

MISS M. (*to* CHAS. P.) Upon my word, Charles, I hardly know where I am. I never expected this; what does it all mean? Is it real?

CHAS. P. I'm not in the conspiracy, I assure you, Cecilia; it's all my uncle's doing. 'Pon my word, he's turning out a regular brick, eh?

Mr. M. Very generous to be sure, but really, I don't like, my dearest Cecilia——

Mrs. M. Nonsense, my dear Cecil. I'm sure that Charles's uncle would feel quite affronted if——

Enter another Servant.

All. Well, what next?

Serv. A coach-builder from Long-Acre has called, with Mr. Henry Percival's compliments, to know when Miss Montagu will be pleased to give her orders for carriages.   [*Exit.*

Chas. P. This is beyond everything! My dear old uncle is coming out strong. (*Aside.*) I always thought he'd got plenty of tin in the background.

Enter Mr. Percival, *as if from a walk, with a brown-paper parcel under his arm. They all advance to greet him, which he seems to resent.*

Mr. P. (*scratching his ear, and dropping the parcel, which every one runs to pick up, Cecilia being first.*) Ah! thankee; it's only a lobster I've bought for my supper. Wasn't dear at a shilling! (*whistles to himself*).

Mrs. M. My dearest sir, we're all much overcome by your great kindness——

Mr. P. Oh! they sent, did they? I thought about this time it would be all right. Lucky escape!

MRS. M. How? What?

MR. P. (*pulling the evening newspaper out of his pocket, and dropping the lobster again, which falls out of the paper.*) Why, that what-d'ye-call-him—turns out to be—one of the Fenian Centres (*sensation*). —A reward of £500 for his apprehension—(*reads from paper*)—Concerned in a murderous assault on a young gentleman at Streatham a few nights since——

ALL. Charles!

MRS. M. He was one of the men who attempted our precious Charles's life! Horrible villain! I always had my suspicions.

MISS M. (*much agitated*) Oh! Charles, Charles!

CHAS. P. (*vehemently*) Why was I so blind? I could have sworn it was Honeywood. I recognised his voice, half stupefied as I lay on the ground, and tried to recollect where I had seen that peculiar stealthy tread before, but I was too weak from loss of breath. The ruffian in front held a gag in my mouth, while his confederate did his best to throttle me from behind (*sensation*).

MR. P. (*deliberately*) May I resume?

MR. M. What else does the paper say?

MR. P. It appears that this Honeywood owes his capture to the confession of one Chorley, a publican in the Borough——

MR. M. (*interrupting*) By God!—pardon the

exclamation, but I can't help it—I was repeating
the particulars of the capture of Chorley to Honeywood himself the other day only, and I observed
that he seemed confused, and changed colour a
little! And he was the accomplice, after all, of
this Chorley?

MR. P. May I resume? (MR. M. *bows assent.*)
Oh! I see that's all.

MR. M. (*smiling*) Ah, well, well. This is a
most singular affair—what I call a providential
deliverance. I wonder what'll be the end of that
fellow——

MR. P. A rope's, if he has his deserts. (*Moves
to go.*)

CHAS. P. It was very lucky that my uncle got
him off to the *Golden Fleece* at Zurich!

MR. M. Most providential. A capital device !·
(*To* MR. P.) Allow me, my dearest friend, to
thank you in all our names for saving my beloved
daughter from ruin. (*He grasps* MR. P.'s *hand,
and* MISS M. *rushes up and throws her arms round
his neck, and kisses him in silence.*) Well, my dear
sir, I hope you'll stay dinner this evening; I can
drive you up in the morning. We never dress
(MRS. *and* MISS M. *exchange looks*), and there is a
bed at your service.

MR. P. (*huskily*) Thankee, no; not very well
—let me see—ah, much obliged (MISS M. *hands*

him his lobster)—shall have it for supper,—and then retire to my couch. (*Mutters to himself:*) Ah! Carriages—say two, £450; Indian shawl, £50—£500; rings, say four, £150—£650; Rimmel's account, £37, 14*s.* 3*d.*; £687, 14*s.* 3*d.* What's his name—Charles's outfit, and a lot of confounded et ceteras, £250—say, £1000. By Jingo! I must retrench. (*Aloud.*) Well, good day to ye; I'm off to-morrow to Vichy.

MRS. M. But, my dearest sir, you'll be present at the marriage?

ALL. Of course, of course.

MR. P. Eh? what marriage? (CHAS. P. *tears his hair.*)

MR. M. (*pleasantly*) Why, of Charles and Cecilia!

MR. P. Ah! I'll see. Stop, let me make a memo of it, or I may forget. (*Takes out a pocket-book.*) When is it, then?

MRS. M. My dearest sir, we cannot fix these things with absolute certainty off-hand. In about a fortnight, Cecil, should you not say?

MR. M. If you say so, my dear——

MR. P. About—a—fortnight—Marriage—Montagu—Iniquitous extortions of infernal revenue—deed of gift—annuity to self—(*Puts book in his pocket.*) That'll do; good morning.

[*Exit whistling.*

CHAS. P. (*apologetically*) I fear you'll think my uncle awfully odd in his manner?

ALL. Oh, no, no.

MR. M. He's a kind-hearted, generous, and honourable man, like his noble and dear brother, the friend of my youth; it's only his way, and between ourselves I take him to be a very rich fellow.

MRS. M. I quite worship eccentricity, for my part. (*Aside.*) I burn to see those rings. What a dear man!

CHAS. P. (*aside*) The most remarkable case of table-turning I ever knew! (*Aloud.*) My uncle only pretends to be indifferent; he will be with us on the joyful occasion.

R. M. He was a good hand at speechifying, I remember, in his younger days.

MR. M. Ah! then he'll be an acquisition at the breakfast. We may look for some dry fun!

MRS. M. (*who has not quite heard*) It seems to be a very serious matter. Fun, indeed! With all his little faults, he was a gentleman by birth, and heir to a peerage, (*aside*) which is more than *some* people can say. (*The rest smile.*)

MISS M. (*in a whisper*) Charles!

CHAS. P. (*bending down to her*) What is it, dear?

MISS M. (*in a whisper*). Oh! I'm so, so happy! (*He squeezes her hand.*)

R. M. My old friend Percival will do the business as neatly as any man I know, when he proposes, ahem! the health of the, ahem! young couple, ahem!

Mr. M. Why, Ralph, what a fellow you are with your *Hems!* There's another toast comes into my mind, that some one will have to name, and we shall all have to drink — Long success to Montagu——

Chas. P. Brothers! Hurrah! So say I.

Mr. M. Not so fast, my young friend. What do you take me for? No, no; what I was going to say, was — Long success — and' (*turning to audience*) I hope you will join us in this — to Montagu and Co.

CURTAIN.

THE END.

Printed by Ballantyne, Hanson & Co.
Edinburgh and London

BY THE SAME AUTHOR

Just published, in one volume, crown 8vo, cloth, price 6s.

LEISURE INTERVALS

I. EARLY POEMS.

II. POEMS WRITTEN BETWEEN 1866 AND 1876.

III. LATER POEMS.